D0059366

THE FINE ART OF MURDER

A murder can be as delicious and titillating as a glass of rare vintage champagne or as pedestrian and bland as a vanilla malted. This volume is concerned only with the former—deaths contrived with loving thought and meticulous planning, masterpieces of murder perpetrated only by those willing to execute their missions with **savoir faire** and extraordinary skill.

Be they amateurs or professionals, nosy landladies or successful thespians, uncles, wives or sons. . . . be their motives money, revenge or love. . . . they will not fail to inspire even the most jaded of crime afficionados.

ANTISOCIAL REGISTER

ALFRED HITCHCOCK

A DELL MYSTERY

Published by DELL PUBLISHING CO., INC.
750 Third Avenue, New York, N.Y. 10017

Copyright © 1965 by H.S.D. Publications, Inc.
Dell ® TM 681510, Dell Publishing Co., Inc.
All rights reserved
First Dell Printing—October 1965   Printed in U.S.A.

ACKNOWLEDGMENTS:

"Tune Me In" by Fletcher Flora—© 1960 by H. S. D. Publications, Inc. Reprinted by permission of the author and the author's agents, Scott Meredith Literary Agency, Inc.

"A Question of Ethics" by James Holding—© 1960 by H. S. D. Publications, Inc. Reprinted by permission of the author and the author's agents, Scott Meredith Literary Agency, Inc.

"The Trap" by Stanley Abbott—© 1964 by H. S. D. Publications, Inc. Reprinted by permission of the author and the author's agents, Scott Meredith Literary Agency, Inc.

"A Habit for the Voyage" by Robert Edmond Alter—© 1964 by H. S. D. Publications, Inc. Reprinted by permission of Scott Meredith Literary Agency, Inc. and Larry Sternig Agency.

"The Empty Room" by Donald Honig—© 1959 by H. S. D. Publications, Inc. Reprinted by permission of Theron Raines.

"I'll Go with You" by Hal Dresner—© 1962 by H. S. D. Publications, Inc. Reprinted by permission of the author and the author's agents, Scott Meredith Literary Agency, Inc.

"The Watchdogs of Molicotl" by Richard Curtis—© 1964 by H. S. D. Publications, Inc. Reprinted by permission of the author and the author's agents, Scott Meredith Literary Agency, Inc.

"The Affair Upstairs" by Helen Nielsen—© 1961 by H. S. D. Publications, Inc. Reprinted by permission of the author and the author's agents, Scott Meredith Literary Agency, Inc.

"I'm Better Than You" by Henry Slesar—© 1961 by H. S. D. Publications, Inc. Reprinted by permission of Theron Raines.

"A Simple Uncomplicated Murder" by C. B. Gilford—© 1959 by H. S. D. Publications, Inc. Reprinted by permission of the author and the author's agents, Scott Meredith Literary Agency, Inc.

"Dead Drunk" by Arthur Porges—© 1959 by H. S. D. Publications, Inc. Reprinted by permission of the author and the author's agents, Scott Meredith Literary Agency, Inc.

"The Last Autopsy" by Bryce Walton—© 1961 by H. S. D. Publications, Inc. Reprinted by permission of Theron Raines.

"One Man's Family" by Richard Hardwick—© 1963 by H. S. D. Publications, Inc. Reprinted by permission of the author and the author's agents, Scott Meredith Literary Agency, Inc.

"You Can Trust Me" by Jack Ritchie—© 1961 by H. S. D. Publications, Inc. Reprinted by permission of Scott Meredith Literary Agency, Inc. and Larry Sternig Agency.

CONTENTS

INTRODUCTION Alfred Hitchcock

I SHOULD LIKE to preempt this space to promote a pet project.

As everyone knows, I'm the last soul to balk at anything that advances the gory, the ghastly, the ghoulish or the gruesome. Whenever called on to endow a new horror magazine or endorse a hideous new product, I've virtually bled myself white with generosity. As high as my fortunes have risen, I've never hesitated to offer a word or two of encouragement to some humble hatchet murderer or stomp killer along the way.

This being the case, it will come as a surprise to my disciples to learn that I favor the abolition of Halloween. But surprise or not, I have powerful lobbies in key places urging that it be stricken from the calendar and another occasion substituted. For no right-thinking adult can help but agree that it has become a crashing bore. Only Father's Day surpasses it for sheer tedium and hypocrisy.

Although Halloween's origins are obscured in the murk of prehistory, it is generally agreed that it has its roots in Roman and Druid harvest festivals. The reaping of summer's bounty signaled the onset of winter, which, as anyone with a poetic turn of mind can tell you, is another way of saying the death of nature.

The Forces of Darkness thus got the upper hand officially on Halloween and celebrated their triumph by running amuck over the countryside. Gremlins and goblins, kites and harpies, witches and poltergeists, warlocks, hammer-locks and bellylocks spread terror and dismay among the bumpkins, which were known among the Romans as rump-kins and among the Druids as drumpkins. These high-jinks picked up virulence around Saturnalia time, continued through the Ides of March, and didn't abate until the official days of the rebirth of nature—Mother's Day. Then the evil spirits went underground and thought up new bits for next autumn.

These frightful goings-on were somewhat modified in the sixth century, when Bombazine the Serene, a Druid patri-arch, set up Thanksgiving Day as a buffer. He shrewdly saw that this holiday would break the momentum of winter-long festivities, so that only a few hardy devils would survive to make the New Year's Eve scene. Walpurgisnacht is also in this, but I can't stop to explain how.

The custom of playing pranks on Halloween arose when humans, jealous (as usual) of the powers possessed by supernatural elements, longed to wreak the same kind of havoc on person and property. This envy, coupled with the energy liberated by the end of harvest and lubricated by the wines and grain liquors abundant in that season, inspired the rural populace to make a great variety of mischief. Fore-most of this was what we now know as "Trick or Treat."

The word "Trick" has its root in the Greek *trichinos*, "of hair" and "Treat" is based on the Latin *tractare*, "to handle." It is clear, then, that the custom goes back to the time when celebrants would call on homes and yell, "Hair or Handle!" at the occupants. It doesn't make much sense to us, but then little about those days does.

Well, things went along pretty much in this vein for a thousand years or so, with only the Crusades and the Sino-Japanese War intervening. These halcyon days were to come to an abrupt end, however, with the advent of the United States. At that point the worst in human nature, which had thankfully prevailed for almost all of recorded history, ran smack dab into conditions totally alien to the flourishing of evil. What it is about the U.S.A. that makes perfectly respectable holidays go a little wiggy when they reach our shores, I don't pretend to know, and besides it is irrelevant to the scope of this study.

I won't detail the atrocities my chums and I used to commit, but I will say that in my day boys showed an astounding genius for increasing the amount of misery in the world, and the varieties of it. When we rapped on a man's door and hollered, "Trick or Treat!" we expected to be "treated" to nothing less than the contents of his wall safe or its equivalent in pastry. Failing this, we perpetrated "tricks" on the scale of the commando raid on Dieppe or the Sepoy Mutiny. Halberds, longbows, maces, corrosive acids, parangs, bolas, becketts, waddies and garrotes were just a few of the implements of our vengeance. When we returned home we left behind us a scene resembling a seaside community after a tidal wave, with cars nestled in trees and railroad tracks twisted like hairpins around telephone poles.

In contrast to this, let us look in on a typical modern community on All Hallow's Eve.

For several weeks the local merchants have been stocking their shelves both with the impedimenta of terrorism and the wherewithal for defending against it. Businessmen have always been opportunists in times of civil disturbance, and they are no different on this occasion. They favor neither side and encourage both. The supermarkets are no-man's-lands where foes mingle around a single source of supply.

In the offensive arsenal we find such dreaded weapons as these: cheesecloth costumes representing witches, monsters, hobgoblins, and such irrelevancies as pirates, nurses and field mice; gauze masks of vampires, skulls, black cats and reigning television celebrities. In addition there are brightly designed shopping bags for the collection of loot. And of course the inevitable boxes of chalk, in gentle pastel shades.

On the defense side, we have matériel calculated either

to frighten or placate wicked imps, and this includes cardboard skeletons and similar hexes, papier-mâché pumpkins with or without electric bulbs, and immense stores of candy stamped in shapes of familiar figures of demonology, including Dracula, Old Harry, Quasimodo and Donald Duck. Everything is displayed in the approved way of merchandising goods, and all products are arranged so as to put the least strain on the imagination.

Since mothers buy the things children use on Halloween, it is small wonder that harmlessness characterizes the holiday. In fact, safety is the theme, and everyone conspires to make sure that nobody is hurt, frightened or even vaguely discomfited.

Selected walls are provided by the Chamber of Commerce for children to deface with chalk. Boys and girls are told that scaring adults could result in heart attacks, and since no child wants to bear for life the responsibility of an adult's death, he restricts his haunting to well-modulated, apologetic moans. Drivers are alerted to proceed with more than usual caution, because the little terrorists can't see approaching cars out of the corners of their masks. Further to this end, phosphorescent insignia are sewn on sleeves and pants legs. Policemen are called out on special service, not to prevent violence and plundering but to help marauders cross the streets. Parties are thrown to keep them off the streets altogether, and games are provided, such as ducking for apples, to help them vent their diabolic urges.

The small and hardy nucleus of children not intimidated by anxious parents stalks the streets raising a kind of hell peculiar to twentieth-century American children. Disguised as ghosts, field mice or Ben Caseys, they go from door to door lisping, "Trick or Treat" with full expectation of cooperation, and without the least idea of what to do if they meet with resistance. But there is never resistance, and cooperation is abundantly given. Mothers and fathers greet them cooing and gurgling over their costumes and ardently pressing chicken-corn, halvah and late-vintage pennies upon them. The operation is brief and streamlined, and if there is either pleasure or pain in the exchange it's almost impossible to detect. But the children, having taken all this for granted, dump their booty into their particolored shopping bags and toddle along to their next victim.

Thus, in a manner of speaking, we can say that Halloween is a very perilous night indeed. At no other time is the danger to healthy youth more apparent. We seem to have forgotten that three prominent elements of a child's psychology are imagination, defiance, and destructiveness. Give a child an educational game and, if he has any spirit at all, he'll quickly destroy the game and find endless, interesting things to do with the box it came in.

Children don't want cooperation and supervision on Halloween; they want to be challenged every step of the way. They don't want treats unless it costs the donor something in mental anguish. They don't want monitored parties or well-lighted streets; they don't want prefabricated costumes or specially designated places where they can destroy worthless property. They simply want to raise hell.

I'm not taking the position that children are pure monsters, because I'm wise enough to know that nothing is pure in this world. But I do think it's vital that we recognize a strong tendency in every normal, healthy child to be uncivilized. Halloween gives him an excellent chance to exercise the antisocial attitudes he's contained the rest of the year. If we suppress these completely, we'll be stopping up a vital source of creativity. This can lead to high-school dropouts, heavy drinking, radical socialism, thirty-one percent more cavities, botulism and premature baldness. Let us therefore restore this holiday to its former position of indignity and disrespect. Or else let's find a suitable alternative. We have a Mother's Day and a Father's Day, so the best substitute would be Children's Day, completing the trend toward child-worship that has been going on since child-labor laws liberated the flower of our youth.

—ALFRED HITCHCOCK

TUNE ME IN Fletcher Flora

"WAKE UP," the voice said.

Freda opened her eyes and looked at the ceiling and waited for the voice to continue, but it was silent. This was not in the least disturbing, however, for sometimes it did not speak to her for hours and hours on end, and then it would speak suddenly, at some odd moment, with specific instructions to do this or that in a particular way at such and such a time. In the beginning the voice had frightened Freda, in the very beginning, but she had soon understood that there was nothing at all to be frightened of, quite the contrary, and she had begun waiting for the voice and listening for it, but she never knew when it would speak. Sometimes it spoke to her when she was quite alone, but at other times it would speak when she was in company, even when she was herself speaking to someone else, and then she would have to quit speaking, perhaps in the middle of a sentence, and listen intently to what the voice said. This was always disconcerting to the other person, of course, the one she was speaking to, and it was really very amusing, in a sense, a kind of comic situation to be laughed at silently.

A strange thing about it was that the voice, although it spoke quite clearly, was never heard by anyone but herself. Another strange thing, even stranger, was that it was never necessary to answer the voice aloud, but only to think quite deliberately the words she wanted heard, and the voice heard them and answered them, and so it was possible to carry on conversations, quite long ones sometimes, without being overheard by anyone else who might be present. These things were strange, however, only in the sense that they were exceptional, undoubtedly beyond the belief of someone who had never experienced them, but they were really conceivable realities. There was nothing supernatural about them, like the presence of light in darkness and a world of sound below the level of hearing.

It was the voice that had brought her to this city, where she had arrived last night, and to this room in this hotel, where she had just awakened. The voice told her what to do, exactly when and how, but she knew perfectly well what she must do in the end, after all the little things that must be done before, and it was to do this, the thing that must be done, that she had come to this place at this time. She had come to kill a man named Hugo Weis.

"You had better get out of bed," the voice said.

It was a gentle reminder. There was in the voice no trace of anger at her lethargy, nor even a suggestion of impatience. The voice was always gentle, always soft, and it was, in truth, a voice of poignant beauty, with a whisper of sadness running through the sounds of vowels and consonants like the slightest soughing of wind among trees at dusk.

"Yes," she thought. "I'd better."

She arose and went into the bathroom and turned on a light. Her face reflected in the mirror above the lavatory seemed somehow the face of another person, not of a stranger but of a person she had known a long time ago in another place and could not now clearly remember. She felt sorry for the face, for the person it belonged to, and she wanted suddenly to cry and tell the face how sorry she was. Instead, she took off her pajamas and showered and went back into the bedroom and dressed and began to brush her hair. She sat on the edge of the bed and brushed with short, quick strokes, her head tilted first to one side and then the other, and as she brushed she began to think about the voice, which did not now respond to her thoughts, and about Hugo Weis, whom she was going to kill.

The voice had told her so, the very first time it had spoken to her, at the same time she had first become aware of Hugo Weis as a monstrous evil. She had been critically ill, had endured extreme fevers, and after her illness there was nothing much to do during a long recuperative period, except to think and read and wait for the long days and nights to pass, and on the morning of this particular day she had opened a newspaper that had been brought to her room by her mother, and there on the front page was a picture of Hugo Weis. She had known about him before, of course, for everyone knew about Hugo Weis, but it was the first time she had ever seen a picture of him, or at least the first time she had ever been really aware of seeing one. He was being investigated by a grand jury for his connections with a vice ring, supposedly international, and there under the black banner of the story was this picture. Only his head and shoulders were shown, and the picture must surely have been blown up from a shot snapped on a street or somewhere by an alert photographer, for Hugo Weis never would have sat for a studio portrait or have voluntarily permitted his picture to be taken anywhere.

He was incredibly ugly, which was not in itself anything to condemn him for, but his ugliness was abnormal, almost terrifying. His face, she thought, was a gross obscenity. Sitting there in her room and staring at the picture, she had studied intently the flat nose with exposed nostrils like black holes burned through the flesh, the mouth like a raw sore about to bleed, the coarse skin pocked by disease. The eyes were almost completely hidden behind lowered lids. She felt in her own flesh a cold and subtle crawling, and she wondered how a man so monstrously marked by evil ugliness could have acquired in his way so much power over other men. It was then, as she wondered, that the voice spoke to her for the first time.

"Hugo Weis must die," the voice said, "and you must kill him."

She had known instantly that it was no hallucination. The voice was real. She could hear it. It spoke clearly and softly from a point just behind her right ear, and it would have been futile to try to convince herself, even if she had wanted to, that it was no more than an echo of her own thoughts. And so, after the first shock of fear and wonder, she accepted the voice quite calmly, almost as if she had been expecting it unconsciously all these years, had been waiting for it to come.

"Why is it I who must kill him?" she wondered.

"Because it is you who have finally answered me."

"Will no one else listen?"

"It's not a question of listening. It's a question of hearing."

"Am I, alone in all the world, the only one who can hear you?"

"You are the first, at least."

"What gives me the power to hear you, and you the power to make me hear? Has my recent illness had anything to do with it?"

"I don't know the answer to your questions. What is the explanation of any miracle, except that it is not a miracle at all, but only the rare effect of natural causes we don't understand? I speak and you hear and that's enough."

"Who is speaking to me?"

"I can't tell you."

"Why?"

"Because I don't know that, either. I am, as a voice, merely the expression of an unconscious imperative. I express the imperative, but I can't have knowledge of the source from which it has sprung."

"I'm not sure I understand."

"Never mind. I'll speak to you again later."

That was the beginning of her relationship with the voice. She had never thought about killing anyone before and it was truly remarkable how she had been able to begin thinking about it, with a kind of detached serenity, as if it were someone else thinking and planning, someone else entirely who listened to the voice and lived at ease with thoughts of violent death. There was apparently no hurry, however. The voice did not urge her or force her to commitments she was not prepared to make. She began in a rather leisurely way to gather all the information she could find on Hugo Weis, and there was very little to be found and still less to be relied upon, for Hugo Weis was elusive, preferring to operate through others while remaining in the heavy shadows of obscurity. He was the son of a laborer. By cunning, treachery and Machiavellian ruthlessness, all working through a strangely compelling personality in an ugly, stunted body, he had made himself the greatest power in the state. He controlled the city in which he lived. He controlled the governor of the state and most of its lawmakers. There were men of consequence in Washington who listened carefully when he spoke. And he spoke always in whispers, behind his hand. The grand-jury investigation never came to anything, of course. One witness died in unusual circumstances, another lost his memory, and another disappeared. In any event, it was doubtful that an indictment would have been returned.

It was in the spring that it all began, and that summer the voice kept returning, speaking to her when it pleased, with no consistency of time or place. In the fall, she resumed her duties as teacher of a sixth grade class in an elementary school near her home, and occasionally the voice visited her during school hours, which sometimes turned out to be embarrassing. It was necessary to become instantly quite still in order to hear what the voice said, it spoke so softly, and these periods of sudden withdrawal, in which she sat or stood as immobile as stone in an attitude of intent listening, were noticed, naturally, by the students. She was afraid that she was gaining a reputation of being odd, but it was impossible to explain that her apparent lapses were actually quite normal and necessary, for no one would have understood, and after awhile she found that it no longer mattered what anyone thought about her.

By this time there was no doubt, if there had ever been any, that she would eventually kill Hugo Weis. She did not feel messianic about it. It was simply something that had to be done. For awhile the possible consequences to herself were disturbing, even frightening, but soon she found herself unable to think beyond the act of killing, as if her own life would also end in that instant and make her eternally invulnerable to earthly harm. It amused her at night, lying in her bed in her dark room, to think of Hugo Weis, wherever he was, doing whatever he might be, completely unaware that he would surely soon die by the hand of a woman he had never seen and would never really know. It was amusing, very amusing, and she laughed softly to herself in the darkness, a whisper of sound in the still room. The face of Hugo Weis floated above her like an ectoplasmic obscenity, ugly and evil.

In March she bought a gun, a 32 caliber revolver, explaining to the local hardware dealer from whom she bought it that it would give her a sense of security, even though she had never fired a revolver in her life. Since she and her mother lived alone in a large house, she said, it seemed unwise to be without any kind of protection at all. The dealer agreed and suggested that she practice firing the revolver in the country Sunday afternoons. He sold her several boxes of cartridges for the revolver, and she carried the revolver and the cartridges home and put them away carefully in a drawer of the dressing table in her room. She did not practice firing the revolver Sunday afternoons, however, for it wasn't necessary. Whatever was necessary would be taken care of in its own time.

Early in June, soon after school was let out for the summer, the long period of waiting came to an end. It ended abruptly, without warning, one afternoon in the reading room of the public library. Freda had gone there for no particular reason, except that the public library was a

pleasant place to be, quiet and restful with sunlight slanting
in through high windows, and she had been going there
regularly for almost as long as she could remember. She was
sitting alone at a table by a window, a book open before
her, but she was not concentrating, was only dimly conscious of words between long intervals of dreaming, and
she could not later remember the name of the book or anything in it that she had read.

"It's time now to do it," the voice said softly and suddenly.

"What?" she thought.

"It's time to kill Hugo Weis. We have waited long
enough."

"How?"

"With the gun. Didn't you buy the gun?"

"Yes. The gun and cartridges."

"Good. It will be quite simple, really. You'll see."

"What should I do?"

"First you must go to the city where he is, of course."

"What then?"

"Go to a hotel. Later, at the right time, you will go to his
office. He sees all sorts of people there, mostly people who
come for favors, and no one will think it odd that you have
come too. Have you learned where the office is?"

"Yes. It's on the south side of the city, near the railroad
station. On Euclid Street."

"So it is. I see you have been preparing yourself well."

"Won't I have trouble getting in to see him?"

"Probably none at all. He makes a point of trying to see
personally all the supplicants who come to him. It's a trick.
He sustains much of his power that way."

"What will happen to me afterward?"

"Never mind that. Don't worry about anything."

Having asked the question, what would happen to her
afterward, she felt for an instant a terrible fear, but in the
next instant the fear had passed, and she arose and returned the book to the stacks and left the library. Home,
she told her mother that she had decided to go up to the

city for a day or two, which was something she had done occasionally ever since she had been old enough, and then she went upstairs to her room and at once began to pack the loaded gun and a few things in a small bag. She had no feeling of having come to a point of crisis in her life, not the beginning of anything or the end of anything or even a radical change from what had been. There was a train, she knew, that left for the city at five o'clock, and having packed and said good-by to her mother, she called a taxi and reached the station with several minutes to spare.

That was yesterday and last night, and now here she was in a room of the hotel to which she'd come, and it was, she saw by her watch, nine o'clock in the morning. She stopped brushing her hair and stood up and put on the light coat she had worn on the train. After putting on the coat, she stood quietly with her head bent forward in a posture of abstraction, as if, now that she was prepared to leave, she had forgotten where she was going or for what purpose. Then, moving all at once, she took the loaded revolver from the small traveling bag and put it in her purse and went out into the hall and downstairs. She walked down, ignoring the elevator, and she walked slowly, not like one reluctant to reach a destination, but with a kind of implicit aimlessness suggesting no destination at all.

She had, in fact, plenty of time. It was over a mile from the hotel to the office of Hugo Weis, and it would not be wise, she thought, to get there too early. From the lobby of the hotel, she passed into a coffee shop and sat down at a small table in the rear. A waitress came with a breakfast menu, but she was not in the least hungry, although she had not eaten since noon of the day before. She ordered only a cup of coffee. She drank the coffee so slowly that it was quite cold before it was half gone, and then she sat on over the cold cup for another ten minutes before leaving. By that time it was just past nine-thirty.

Reaching Euclid Street, carrying the purse under her arm and still walking with the implicit aimlessness of one with no place in particular to go, she turned south in the direction of Hugo Weis's office. She could not recall exactly how she had learned where the office was. Probably it was something she had known for a long time. It was a rather famous location, after all, and had received a lot of publicity at various times. It was the first office Hugo Weis had ever had, two dark rooms in a shabby building in a poor section, and it was evidence of his great vanity that he had remained there all these years, exercising his swollen power and gathering a fortune in the same place where he had begun. It was another trick, she thought. A lie. An illusion of humility sustained by a monster of conceit.

Walking along the street, she felt wonderfully good, almost exhilarated. She felt, indeed, rather gaseous, hardly touching the concrete pavement with her feet, on the verge of rising and floating away with every step. She had felt this way sometimes as a girl, especially early in the morning of a spring day when she had got up ahead of all the others and gone alone into the yard. And there in the window of a department store was a thin dress of palest blue that was just the kind of dress for the effervescent girl that she had been and now wasn't. She stopped in front of the window and gazed at the dress for several minutes, clutching under her arm the purse, and the gun in the purse, and then she turned away and walked on and came pretty soon to the certain shabby building in the poor section. On the street outside the building, as she waited before entering, the voice spoke to her for the next to the last time it ever would. As always, it was a voice of poignant beauty, with a whisper of sadness running through it.

"Here you are at last," the voice said. "It took a long time."

"Yes," she thought. "A long time."

She continued to wait, her head inclined and cocked a little to one side, but the voice did not speak again, and after a minute or two she crossed to the entrance of the building and went into a dark hallway from which a narrow staircase ascended through shadows to the second floor.

She went up the stairs, hesitating for a moment at the top, then turning back toward the street along a kind of narrow gallery at the edge of the stairwell. There were two doors spaced along the gallery, each with a pane of frosted glass on which nothing was printed. She went past the first to the second, the one nearer the street, and opened it and entered a small room that seemed to make a special point of its drab bareness. The floor was uncovered, blackened and greasy from the application of sweeping compound. A dozen straight chairs stood at intervals against three walls. On one chair sat an old man in a stained and wrinkled seersucker suit, his withered hands twisted together in his lap. On another chair, against the opposite wall, sat a woman with bright yellow hair who was wearing an expensive fur piece around her shoulders and a bored, carefully detached expression on her face.

These two appeared to be the only occupants of the room, but then Freda saw a man behind a desk beside a door in the fourth wall. She crossed to the desk and stood looking down at the man. He had a thin face with a long nose above a lipless line of a mouth. His quality of deadliness was as discernible as scent or sound, and although he was serving as a receptionist, his first function was obviously that of bodyguard. Looking down at him, Freda had a feeling of immeasurable superiority, a singing sense of exhilaration that was the climax of the effervescence she had felt on the way to this place. No one, she thought, could prevent her from doing what she had come to do. No one on earth.

"I would like to see Mr. Weis," she said.

"Your name?"

"Freda Bane."

The man looked up at her with a glitter of contempt in his eyes and down again immediately at his hands lying spread on the desk as if they were fingering silent chords on an invisible keyboard.

"Do you have an appointment?"

"No, but I've come a long way, from out of town, and I

would like to see him only for a few minutes. It's very important."

"It's always important. Always." The man shrugged and folded the fingers of his hands. "Have a chair over there. He'll see you, all right. He sees everyone."

She turned away and sat down on the nearest chair. She sat erect, primly, her ankles together. Her purse lay in her lap under her hands, and she could feel the gun in it. Once she even opened the purse enough to slip a hand inside and touch the naked steel. It was an intensely intimate and exciting gesture, like touching the flesh of someone loved, and she nearly whimpered in the excitement of it. But then she must have become quite abstracted and withdrawn, for after awhile, however much time had passed, she became aware that the old man was gone, and the woman with yellow hair and the fur piece was crossing to the door to the next room and was quickly gone also. She continued to sit primly on the chair, no longer exhilarated as before, but quietly assured in a feeling that was more like resignation than anything else, and very soon the man at the desk looked across at her and jerked his head slightly toward the door behind him.

"You can go in now," he said.

"Thank you," she said.

She wondered what signal he had received to tell him it was time. Perhaps there was a little light on the front of the desk. Something of the sort that made no sound. Standing, her purse held in both hands in front of her, she walked over to the door and into the next room, from which the yellow-haired woman had apparently gone directly into the hall, and there behind an old desk of dark oak beyond six feet of bare floor was Hugo Weis, whom she would shoot dead in exactly sixteen seconds.

He was so short of stature that only his head and shoulders were visible above the desk, but as she moved toward him, he stood up suddenly and came around the desk to meet her, his stunted and gnarled body exposed, his face touched, when he stopped, by the light from a single

window. It was the same face she had seen in the newspaper and floating like an ectoplasmic vision in her dark
room at home, obscenely ugly, except for a single difference
which was now apparent in the weak light, and she was
arrested by this difference, held by it for seconds, and the
difference was in his eyes. They were soft eyes, the eyes of
a grieving woman.

"My name is Freda Bane," she said, feeling in these last
seconds that it was somehow decidedly important that she
identify herself.

When she spoke, it seemed to her that his soft eyes
widened with a kind of shock and filled instantly afterward
with what seemed to her a light of infinite relief. She had a
wild notion that he suddenly recognized her voice, as if it
had materialized from a dream he had often had, but had
never, until now, quite been able to remember after waking.

"Come in," he said. "Come in."

His voice was gentle, compatible with his eyes.

*It was, in truth, a voice of poignant beauty, with a whis-
per of sadness running through the sounds of vowels and
consonants like the slightest soughing of wind among trees
at dusk.*

A QUESTION OF ETHICS James Holding

ON THIS OCCASION, his contact in Rio was a man called
simply Rodolfo. Perhaps Rodolfo had another name, but
if so, Manuel Andradas did not know it. He was to meet
Rodolfo in the Rua do Ouvidor on a corner by the flower
market. While he waited, standing with his back against
a building wall on the narrow sidewalk, he looked with
admiration at a basket of purple orchids being offered for
sale in a flower stall opposite. He wore his camera case
slung prominently over his left shoulder.

Rodolfo, when he brushed past Manuel and murmured
"follow" from the corner of his mouth, proved to be a
nondescript, shabbily dressed man. Manuel followed him
through the noonday crowd to a small cafe. There, over a
cafezinho, they faced each other. Manuel kept his attention
on his tiny cup of jet-black coffee.

Rodolfo said, "Photographer, would you like a little
trip?"

Manuel shrugged.

"To Salvador," Rodolfo said. "Bahía. A beautiful city."

"So I have heard. Is there a deadline?"

"No deadline. But as little delay, Photographer, as possible." Manuel was known to his contacts simply as The

Photographer. He *was* a photographer, in truth. And a good one, too.

"The price?" And as he asked the question, Manuel lifted his muddy brown eyes to Rodolfo, and sipped delicately at his coffee.

"Three hundred thousand *cruzeiros*."

Manuel sucked in his breath. "Your principal must need the work done desperately," he ventured.

Rodolfo smiled, if you could call the oily lift of his lip a smile. "Perhaps," he said. "I do not know. Is it satisfactory?"

"Very generous, yes. Perfectly satisfactory. Expenses, of course, and a third of the price now?"

"*Va bem.*"

The man called Rodolfo idly scratched with a pencil stub on the back of the cafe menu, and turned it toward Manuel. On it, he had written a name and an address. Automatically, Manuel committed them to memory. Then he folded the menu and tore it into tiny pieces and dropped them into the pocket of his neat dark suit. He was frowning.

Watching his expression, Rodolfo said, "What's the matter?"

Manuel said with disapproval, "It's a woman."

Rodolfo laughed. "Business is business, isn't it?"

"I prefer men, that's all," Manuel said.

They rose after draining their coffee cups and turned out into the avenue. Rodolfo, when he shook hands, left a thick pad of currency in Manuel's hand.

Manuel stopped in an open street stall on his way back to his studio and drank a glass of cashew juice. It was better than coffee for settling the nerves, he believed.

Six days later, he went ashore at Bahía from a down-at-the-heels freighter that stopped there on its way north to take on a consignment of cocoa, hides and castorbeans.

Unwilling to invite attention, he walked from the landing place through the teeming traffic of the Baixa to one of the municipal elevators he could see towering against the cliff above the lower town. The elevator lifted him quickly to the Alta and spewed him out into the municipal square of the upper town. From there, he had a magnificent view over the foliage of fire-red flamboyant trees to the harbor below him, with its lively shipping and quiet fortress.

In the shadowed lobby of the Palace Hotel on Rua Chile, he registered for a room under his own name, Manuel Andradas. And for two days thereafter he behaved exactly as a photographer on assignment for a picture magazine might behave. With two cameras draped about him, he visited Bahía's places of interest, taking numerous photographs of everything from the elaborately carved facade of the Church of the Third Order to the Mondrian-like blue and tan egg-crate walls of the new Hotel Bahía. On the third day of his stay, having established for himself in the city the character of a harmless, innocent photographer, he set about his true business in Bahía.

About an hour after noon, he stuffed a pair of swimming shorts into his camera case with his cameras and left the hotel. He walked up Rua Chile to the square where scores of busses were angled into parking slots, bearing with mechanical indifference the deluge of propaganda and music that cascaded upon him from loudspeakers placed around the plaza. He swung confidently aboard a bus that was labeled *Rio Vermelho and Amaralina,* and took a seat at the rear, a sallow, fine-boned man of quite ordinary appearance except for disproportionately large hands and heavily muscled forearms. Not one among the vociferous, pushing passengers that soon filled the bus to overflowing gave him more than a passing glance.

Manuel closed his eyes and thought of the work ahead. He felt the bus start, heard the excited gabble of the passengers, but did not open his eyes. The name, now? He remembered it perfectly. Eunicia Camarra. Yes. The address? Amaralina, Bahía. Yes.

Eunicia Camarra. A woman. What was she, or what had she done, that somebody in Rio—his formless, nameless, unknown "customer" in Rio—should want her nullified?

That was the word Manuel always used to himself: nullified. Was she a faithless mistress, perhaps? A woman who had spurned an offer of marriage? Three hundred thousand *cruzeiros* was a substantial sum. Perhaps a woman of whom his customer—also a woman?—was jealous?

Manuel, of course, never knew the truth about his assignments. After the job was done by whatever means seemed most appropriate and practical to Manuel, he never found out the true reason that his professional services had been required. And that was just as well. He preferred to remain emotionally uninvolved in his work. He did each job quietly and efficiently, and avoided becoming entangled in its moral or ethical ramifications.

He put Eunicia Camarra from his mind and opened his eyes. The bus went inland a little way, giving him brief glimpses of raw red earth, patchy gardens, lush tropical foliage. Then its route took the bus back within sight of the sea again, and he felt a cool ocean breeze, entering through the bus windows, begin to dry the slick of perspiration off his face.

At the Amaralina bus stop, he was deposited beside a thatched, circular shelter house only a few yards from the beach. Directly before him stood a cafe, scrubbed clean of paint by the endless pummeling of wind and blown sand. It had an open terrace facing the beach. Nearby, a man with shiny white teeth smilingly sold coconuts to half a dozen schoolgirls, hacking off the top of the nuts for them with a machete so that they could drink the sweet milk.

The children's voices, gay with school-is-over-for-the-day spirits, rang merrily in Manuel's ears as he walked slowly past the cafe terrace and up the beach to a tumble-down bathing pavilion where he changed into his swimming trunks. Then he took his camera case and went out to the beach.

There were not many people about. He saw one couple lying in the sand behind some outcropping rocks, completely engrossed in each other. He saw a small knot of bathers off to his right, wading knee deep in the foaming surf and emitting shrill cries of pleasure. Far off to his left, he could see the buildings of Ondina hugging the sapphire bay. And before him, close to the water's edge, the same schoolgirls he had noticed buying coconuts, were cavorting in the sand.

He went and sat on the sand near the children, cradling his camera case in his hands. The girls wore a simple blue and white school uniform, he saw, and were approximately of the same age—twelve or thirteen, perhaps. He smiled at them and greeted them gravely, *"Bons dias, senhoritas."* That was all. He didn't push himself forward. He was more subtle than that. When they returned his greeting, they saw the camera case in his hands. And at once, they evinced a lively interest in it, especially the blonde child who seemed to be the leader of the group.

She approached Manuel. "Is there a camera in that case?" she asked. "May we please see it? Will you take our picture? Are your photos in color? What kind of *pellicula* do you find most satisfactory, *senhor?* Will you show me how to adjust the lens so that I may take a photo also?"

This was said so breathlessly, so beguilingly, with such animated childish curiosity, that Manuel laughed in spite of himself and said, "Not quite so fast, *senhorita*, if you please! So many questions all at once! Yes, it contains a camera. Several of them. And yes, you may have a quick look at them, but be careful not to get any grains of sand in them." He held out the camera case and the children clustered around it, chattering and exclaiming. The little girl who had requested the privilege of seeing his camera opened the case.

"Wonder!" she said. "A Leica! It is very expensive, no? My grandmother has one." She delved deeper. "And a baby camera!" she exclaimed, holding up Manuel's Minox. "Such a small camera I have never seen."

Manuel sat quietly in the sand and let the children handle his equipment, keeping an eye on them to prevent damage, however. Then he said, "I shall take a photo of you now, all in your school uniforms." They stood demurely together, smiling while he snapped their picture.

The blonde child said, "Will you send us the picture? My grandmother would like to see it."

"Certainly," Manuel said. "And I shall not charge you for it, though I am a professional photographer and get large sums for my work."

"Oh, thank you, *senhor*," the blonde girl said. Manuel nodded to her, realizing with satisfaction that he had now so ingratiated himself with these children that they would answer eagerly any questions he chose to ask them: questions about Amaralina, their homes, their neighbors, their parents' friends, even questions, no doubt, about a woman named Eunicia Camarra. But there was no hurry.

The blonde child said, "Are you going into the water, *senhor?* If so, we will care for your cameras while you bathe. No harm shall come to them." She appealed to her friends; they chorused agreement.

"Why not?" Manuel said. "If you will be so kind. *Muito obrigado.*" And in rising to enter the water, he made his first mistake. But he was hot and sweaty, and a swim would be welcome, even though he was not a good swimmer. And the girls would remain until he came back, because they would be watching his cameras for him.

"Have a care, there by the rocks," the blonde child said. "There is a strong current there."

He scarcely heard her. His mind was on other things. And only when he had plunged boldly into the water and stroked his way some distance out from shore did he fully comprehend what the child had said. Then it was almost too late. He felt himself in the grip of a force too powerful for even his big hands and muscled arms to resist. His head went under the water and he choked. And he thought, foolishly, how much better to remain hot and sweaty than to cool off at such a price. Then he couldn't think any more at all.

When he opened his eyes, the glaring blue of the sky hurt them. He was lying on his back in the sand. He felt weak, sick. And as he shifted his pained gaze, it centered on the skinny, naked body of the blonde girl standing not far from him, about to drop her grubby uniform dress over her head to cover her wet skin. Near her, as his eyes turned, were two of the other schoolgirls, also engaged in slipping on their dresses over wet bodies. He made a choking, grunting sound and sat up suddenly.

The girls screamed and went on wriggling happily into their dresses. "Do not look, *senhor!*" the blonde child cried gaily. "We must first arrange our clothing! We have been swimming without suits." The other girls' laughing voices joined hers like the twittering of small parrots. Manuel shook his head to clear it, coughing water onto the sand. The little blonde girl was saying, "We warned you, *senhor.* There is a strong undertow. You paid no attention!" She scolded him gently, but he could tell that she was mightily pleased he had ignored her warning so that she and her friends might have the marvelous excitement of saving him from the sea. "We are all excellent swimmers," she continued chidingly, "because we live here in Amaralina. But you are not a good swimmer, *senhor.*" She smiled at him. "But we pulled you out. Maria and Letitia and I." Scornfully she said, "The others ran away."

Now Manuel Andradas felt a wave of a very unfamiliar emotion sweep through him, and he said, "*Senhoritas,* I owe you my life. I am grateful. I thank you from my heart." They were embarrassed.

He looked at the blonde child, who was combing her fingers through her wet taffy-colored hair and asked with a premonition of disaster, "*Come se chama?* What is your name?"

"Eunicia Camarra," she said. "What is yours?"

He sent the other children home with his thanks, but prevailed upon Eunicia to stay a little longer on the beach with him. "I wish to take your picture again," he explained. "Alone. To have a record of the lady who saved my life." And curiously enough, he found himself for the first time in his career regarding a proposed victim with something besides cold objectivity. He felt an unaccustomed lift of his heart when he looked at Eunicia—an emotion compounded of gratitude, admiration, liking and strangest of all, tenderness, almost as though she were his own child, he thought vaguely. At the end, after snapping her in a series of childish, charming poses, he said on an impulse, "Now show me how I looked when you pulled me from the water and dragged me onto the beach."

She laughed delightedly and flopped down like a rag doll on the sand. Her arms were disposed limply at her sides; her legs lay loosely asprawl; the closed eyes in her thin face were turned up to the sky; and her mouth gaped. She looked remarkably like a corpse. Manuel leaned over her then, and used his Minox to snap her like that.

And all the time, they were talking.

"Do you live here with your mother and father?" he asked.

"Oh, no, *senhor* Andradas, my mother and father are dead. I live with my grandmother, in that big house up there on the hill." She waved inland.

"I see. A big house, you say. Your grandmother is a rich woman, I suppose. Not likely to want you saving the life of a poor photographer."

She was indignant. "My grandmother is a great lady," she averred stoutly. "But of course, she is very rich, as you say. After all, when my grandfather was alive, was he not the greatest diamond merchant in Brazil?"

"Was he?"

"So my grandmother says."

"Then I am sure it is true. And you are alone there with your grandmother, eh?" He peered at her with his muddy eyes. "No brothers or sisters or relatives to keep you company?"

"None," she said sadly. Then she brightened. "But I have

a half-brother in Rio. He is an old man now, over thirty I believe, but he is my half-brother nevertheless. His mother was the same as mine," she explained importantly. "But a different father, you see?"

Manuel was, in truth, beginning to see. "Your grandmother does not like your half-brother?" he guessed.

"No. She says he is *malo*. A liar and a cheat and a disgrace to her family. My mother ran away and married when she was too young. And brother Luis was born then. I feel sorry for him, because his father is dead, like mine. I write to him sometimes, but I do not tell my grandmother."

"I can see that you might not want her to know," Manuel agreed gravely.

"Especially when she will not help him, even with money. And he asks her many times, I know. She refuses, always."

"Perhaps she will leave him some money in her will when she dies."

"Oh, no, she will not. I am to have it all. Luis will not get a penny, Grandmother says, while anybody else is alive in the family. She has no patience with brother Luis, you see. Poor Luis. But I think he is quite nice. I shall go to Rio and visit him and do his cooking for him," she finished in a dreaming voice, "when Grandmother gives me enough money."

"You've never seen him?"

"No. Only his picture. He sent me a picture in a letter last year, the one in which he asked whether Grandmother had softened toward him. And I sent him a picture of me when I answered. He's quite handsome, really."

"What is his name?" Manuel said.

"Luis Ferreira."

"Does he have a job?"

"Yes. He works in the office of the Aranha Hotel."

After he had changed out of his swimming trunks in the pavilion, Manuel took Eunicia up to the cafe terrace and, with unaccustomed generosity, bought her a bottle of orange pop. She guzzled the pop energetically. Then she went home, saying her grandmother would be anxious if she didn't soon appear. Manuel said in parting "I am very grateful, Eunicia. Perhaps I shall be able to do you a service in return."

Long after she had gone, he sat alone on the cafe terrace, crouching uncomfortably on a fixed pedestal seat beside a square slate table, and stared out across the beach at the foam-laced sea. He ordered three Cinzanos and drank them down rapidly, one after the other, wrestling with his unexpected problem. Three hundred thousand *cruzeiros!* The whole thing, he thought gloomily, had now come down simply to a question of ethics.

He wished he had a glass of cashew juice.

Manuel Andradas returned to Rio on the night plane that evening. He went from the airport directly to his studio, developed the Minox film he had exposed in Bahía, and carefully examined the tiny negatives with a magnifying glass before selecting one and making a blown-up print of it. He called the anonymous telephone number that eventually put him in touch with the man called Rodolfo, and arranged to meet him again in the Rua do Ouvidor in the morning. Then he went to bed and slept dreamlessly.

Next day, he showed the print to the man called Rodolfo. "It was not a woman," he said with disapproval. "It was a child."

Rodolfo examined the photograph of Eunicia. It showed her lying limp and unquestionably dead on the beach at Amaralina. He nodded with satisfaction. "This should be adequate proof," he said. He kept looking at the picture. Then he smiled. "Even the young donkey sometimes loses its footing," he said sententiously. "May I keep this photograph? It will be passed along to our principal. And if all is well, I shall meet you at the same place tomorrow afternoon at three."

He went off with Manuel's print. And at three the next afternoon, he met Manuel again near the flower market and paused only long enough to shake his hand and say,

"Good work. Satisfactory." This time, he left an even thicker pad of currency in Manuel's hand than when first they had met.

Manuel pocketed the banknotes almost casually, and hailed a taxi. In it, he had himself driven to Copacabana Beach, where he descended about a block from the Aranha Hotel on Avenida Atlantica. Dismissing the cab, he glanced appraisingly at the wide beach, peopled at this hour of the afternoon by bathers as numerous as ants on a dropped sugar cake. Then he entered the public telephone booth across the street, called the Aranha Hotel, and was soon talking in a purposely muffled voice to *Senhor* Luis Ferreira, one of the hotel's bookkeepers.

All he said to him, however, was, "I have a message for you from Bahía, *Senhor* Ferreira. Meet me on the beach across from your hotel in ten minutes. By the kite-seller's stand." He waited for no reply, but hung up and left the booth.

Then he strolled up the beach toward the hotel, automatically picking his way between the thousands of sea and sun worshippers scattered on the sand. Near the small dark man who sold bird-kites to the children he stationed himself, an unnoticed member of the holiday crowd. From the corners of his eyes, he watched the hotel entrance.

Soon a slightly stooped young man with a receding chin and thinning blond hair, came out of the hotel door, dodged through the rushing traffic of the avenue to the beach and approached the kite salesman. He paused there, looking with worried eyes at the people around him. The beach was crowded; any one of all those thousands could be the message-bringer from Bahía. He looked at his wristwatch, gauging the ten minutes Manuel had mentioned. And Manuel was sure, then, that this was Luis Ferreira, and none other—the half-brother of Eunicia Camarra.

Manuel stepped quietly toward him through the hodgepodge of bathers. As he did so, he withdrew his hand from his pocket, and brought out with it, concealed in the palm, a truncated dart of the kind, with a long metal point, that is used to throw at a cork target. The dart had its point filed to a needle sharpness; half the wooden shaft had been cut off, so that the dart handle fitted easily into Manuel's hand with only a half inch of needle projecting. And on the needle's point was thickly smeared a dark, tarry substance.

Several customers were clustered around the kite seller. Four youths were playing beach ball three yards away. A fat man and a thin woman lay on the sand, almost at Ferreira's feet.

Approaching Ferreira, Manuel seemed to stumble over the outthrust foot of the fat sunbather. He staggered a bit, and his heavy boot came down with sickening force on the instep of Luis Ferreira. Manuel threw out his hands as though to catch himself. And in that act, the point of the dart entered deeply into Ferreira's wrist, just below his coat sleeve.

Ferreira did not notice. The prick of the needle was overlooked in the excruciating pain of his trodden instep. He jumped back and cursed. Manuel apologized for his clumsiness and walked on up the beach, losing himself in the crowd within seconds.

He neither hurried enough to be conspicuous, nor lagged enough to waste precious time. Nor did he look back. Not even when he left the beach after a few blocks and walked briskly down Avenida Atlantica toward the city's center, did he so much as turn his head toward where he had left Ferreira. What need? He knew perfectly well what was happening back there.

Already the curare from the dart point would have completed its deadly work. Ferreira's body would be lying upon the beach, still unnoticed, perhaps, among all those reclining figures, but with the motor nerve endings in its striated muscles frozen and helpless, the beating of its heart soon to be forever stilled by the paralyzing drug. In three minutes or less, Ferreira would be dead. That was certain. And the blonde child of Bahía who had so strangely touched the long-dormant buds of affection in Manuel Andradas, was safe from harm.

Manuel permitted himself a chuckle as he walked toward town. If someone saves your life, he thought, you owe them a life in return. And if someone pays for a death, you owe them a death for their money.

He smiled, his muddy brown eyes looking straight ahead.

This question of ethics, he thought, is not so difficult after all.

THE TRAP   Stanley Abbott

THE EMORY SINCLAIRS should have been happy. They owned the house on East 70th Street where they lived in New York, a sumptuous winter home in Palm Beach, and they could hardly count their money.

But Emory Sinclair, having made a fortune before he was thirty-five, was trying to double it before he was forty-five. Helen Sinclair, neglected and bored, spent her days in expensive salons being massaged, beautified or fitted; though she was thirty-six, she appeared to be not a day over thirty.

All might have been well if Emory Sinclair hadn't fired his female secretary. But convinced that all women were congenital idiots, he did so, and took on Paul Fenton. Mrs. Sinclair wasn't slow to notice that the young man was single and attractive.

From a room on the third floor of the house on East 70th, which he called his study, Emory Sinclair dealt in foreign currencies. Moving his vast capital around the world, he gambled on the news of a government about to fall, a dictator assassinated, or the failure of a crop. And he insisted that his private secretary live in.

As well as his normal work, Paul Fenton looked after Mrs. Sinclair's private accounts. As he was good-looking and dressed well, he was often asked to fill in when she needed an odd man for a dinner party. At other times, he was only too glad to take her to a theatre when Emory Sinclair was too busy to go.

It wasn't long before Helen Sinclair's feminine instinct told her what was happening. Paul was amusing, and though she knew she took a risk deceiving Emory, danger added a spice of its own to the adventure.

But what began as a quiet affair blazed into a passion that took them by surprise; it overwhelmed them; they were convinced they couldn't live without each other. Paul would have gone straight to Emory Sinclair and told him, even though it meant losing his job, if Helen Sinclair hadn't restrained him. Though she appeared to be an ordinarily pretty woman, there was a firmness to the delicate chin and a lurking shrewdness behind the soft appeal of her very blue eyes. And she was under no illusions as to what Emory Sinclair's reaction would be if she asked him for a divorce. She had no money of her own, and Paul had his salary only so long as he had his job. Love in a cold-water flat was not for her. Besides, she had no desire to be parted from a fortune which she knew was more than a million dollars.

Over the next few weeks she thought about the problem; in fact, it was never out of her mind. At times she thought she detected a mocking smile on Emory Sinclair's fat pink face, and wondered if he knew and was enjoying the situation; it would be just like him to play cat and mouse. This, added to her frustration, put her in a sullen fury. She found herself playing with ideas for getting rid of him (she didn't like the word "murder"), only she couldn't think of a way that wasn't violent and that would also be foolproof. But Helen Sinclair didn't give up easily, and eventually she hit on an ingenious plan.

It wasn't until the day they were closing up the house on East 70th for the winter that an opportunity presented itself. She was sitting in Emory Sinclair's study on the third floor, waiting while he went over some papers with Paul. In less than an hour they would be leaving. Everything had been done, the furniture had been placed under dustcovers, the luggage was down in the front hall, and the servants had been paid.

Paul came over to her. "Here are your plane tickets, Mrs. Sinclair."

She saw Emory watching her. How she hated that funny mocking smile! She never could tell what he was thinking; an enigma.

"Thank you, Paul," she said, smiling at him graciously.

Emory said, "Paul has to go downtown right away with these papers for the Lazards so I've told Johnson to take him in the car. We won't need it any more. We'll take a taxi to the airport." He turned to Paul. "Tell Barton to have one outside in fifteen minutes."

While Paul was talking on the house phone to the butler, Helen Sinclair was thinking fast. When Paul had gone she would be alone in the house with Emory. She got up and walked to the door. Her heart was beating rapidly but outwardly she was calm as she said, "Then I'll tell Barton he can leave. We won't need him after he's got the taxi."

In her room on the floor below she sat listening. While she waited, she went over in her mind what she would do when Paul had left. It had been arranged that she and Emory would go to the airport together, she to fly to Florida where she would be staying with the Hendersons for a month before she opened their own house in Palm Beach. Emory was flying to Chicago, where he would be staying at the Monahan Club for three weeks, after which time he would be joining her at the Hendersons. Paul was going to Philadelphia to stay with his family. It was perfect. Nothing would be known for three weeks. When Emory didn't show up at the Monahan Club, they would merely think he had changed his plans. By the time he was reported missing it would be too late. What she had to do now was simple, just a matter of timing. When it was all over, one telephone call. It was foolproof.

The thud of the front door brought her to her feet. The car was just pulling away when she got to the window. Now

Paul had gone, all she had to do was get rid of Barton. She hurried to gather up her coat, handbag and gloves. A final glance at the mirror, a touch to the little fur hat to set it more becomingly, and she took the elevator to the ground floor.

"Mr. Sinclair has changed his plans, Barton," she told him. "He isn't going till later. Just leave his bags here in the hall and put mine in the taxi. Tell the driver I'll be out in a few minutes."

Barton came back in and she told him he needn't wait. When he had left she checked the front door to see that it was properly shut.

She looked at her watch. They were to leave at ten-thirty; it was six minutes to the half hour. In a passage that led from the front hall to the kitchens at the rear she turned on the light and opened a cupboard. On the wall were the main electric switches and the fuse panel. On a shelf below the panel was a cardboard box holding an assortment of fuses. She went through them; some were good, some burnt out. She took one that was burnt out and set it on the shelf, then went back to the front hall and stood waiting by the elevator. Around her the house was cold and silent. It seemed like a lifetime standing there. She tried not to think, but her imagination ran riot. When she started to shake, she wondered if she could go through with it.

Suddenly she stiffened as she heard Emory's door slam, then his heavy tread as he stepped into the elevator. When she heard the distant whine of the motor she moved swiftly down the passage to the fuse panel, reached up and pulled out the fuse marked "Elevator." In its place she inserted the one that was burnt out; the good one she dropped into the box, and shut the cupboard doors. She took a deep breath. Now for the part she dreaded most.

As she hurried through the passage she could hear him pounding on the elevator door above. And when she came out into the front hall, the noise thundered down the shaft, drumming in her ears and putting her in a panic. As her heels clattered across the marble floor, the pounding stopped suddenly. She had almost reached the front door when it started up again, reverberating violently through the house, and with it a frantic screaming that struck a chill to her heart. She wrenched the door open, slammed it behind her, and paused on the top step breathing hard, to find the taxi driver staring up at her. *Could he have heard?* she wondered. She listened carefully while pretending to search through her bag. It was impossible to hear anything, and the door had only been open a moment. She took a grip on herself, ran down the steps and into the cab.

"Please hurry," she gasped, "or I'll miss my flight."

On the plane she took a sleeping pill and told the stewardess she didn't want to be disturbed. When she awoke they were over Florida. The Hendersons met her at the airport and, in brilliant sunshine, they drove out to their house on the beach.

For the next few days Helen Sinclair tried not to think. She swam, played tennis or went shopping. She was never alone. At night there was always a party somewhere, and when she went to bed she took sleeping pills. She was able to keep her conscience at bay. On the sixth night she dreamed someone was pounding on her bedroom door; she fought her way to it but when she tried to open it the knob came away in her hand. The pounding went on unceasingly. Frantic with terror she kicked and clawed at the door. It was as immovable as a solid block of marble.

She awoke screaming and wringing wet. For some time she sat up in bed listening. The house was silent. No one had heard. The question she had been pushing away for days shot into the forefront of her mind. Was he dead yet? She couldn't dodge it; her mind had a life of its own utterly beyond control. With dreadful clarity she saw Emory trapped in the elevator, screaming for help, crouched on the floor, kicking at the door; and slowly, inexorably, dying.

She couldn't stand it any longer. If only she could tell somebody. She stared at the telephone on the night table, wondering if she dare speak to Paul. She picked it up and dialed Long Distance, but before the operator could answer she hung up. It was too dangerous. She realized it was something she was going to have to keep to herself, always. With each day that passed, Helen Sinclair's mind became easier. After three weeks, what had happened had slipped into the past and no longer troubled her.

The Hendersons were giving a party for her that night. It was her birthday. She was driving to the hairdresser's with Lois Henderson when Lois asked, "What time will Emory be down?"

She gave a start. She had almost forgotten it was today he was supposed to join her.

"Some time this afternoon, I guess," she replied.

"Well, if he's like my old man," Lois said, "he'll remember it's your birthday next year."

She laughed. "That's Emory alright."

She remembered with wry amusement how a couple of months before they had looked at a lovely emerald necklace; Emory had said it was too expensive. She promised to buy it for herself when she got back to New York.

In the afternoon she went up to her room to rest before the party and went over in her mind what she would do when Emory hadn't shown up. She would let the Hendersons see she was worrying but she wouldn't do anything about it till the next day. Then she would call the Monahan Club in Chicago and Paul in Philadelphia. She would tell Paul she was returning to New York, and call Barton to open the house on East 70th. And she would ask Paul to report Emory as missing. It would all work out very nicely. By the time she got there, the unpleasant part would be over. She gave herself up to daydreams of Europe and Paul and a quiet wedding.

Later, when she had dressed and gone downstairs, she went into the living room and came face to face with Emory Sinclair. She stood rooted, feeling the blood rush away from her face. She was sure she was going to faint. She tried to speak. Her lips moved but made no sound. He was standing with a glass in his hand, staring at her with that funny mocking smile.

"Hello, Helen," he said, "you look as if you'd seen a ghost."

She stared back at him, speechless, wondering what had happened. He couldn't have got out. It must have been the taxidriver—or Barton. That was it—Barton. He was the only one who had a key. Perhaps he'd forgotten something and gone back to the house She fell into a chair.

"I'm not well," she tried to say, but it came out in a faint whisper.

Emory turned to the bar without a word, poured a drink and came back with it. It was straight Scotch. She drained it.

"Don't try to talk," he said, and sitting opposite her lit a cigar.

She sat quietly, feeling her strength slowly returning, and watching him from beneath her lashes, tried to read his face. *He's going to keep me guessing,* she thought.

"You look better," he said after a while. "Could you stand a surprise?" He was leaning forward, watching her, but she didn't say anything.

He put his cigar in an ashtray and reached into a coat pocket.

"I didn't forget it this time." His hand came out holding a black case. He held it out to her and flipped the lid open. "Take it," he said.

She reached out hesitantly. On a bed of white satin lay an emerald necklace. She looked at it, then back to him, puzzled, scanning his face.

"When did you . . . "

"I got it when I went downtown the morning we left. I wanted to get it before flying out to Chicago."

"You went downtown?" she heard herself asking.

"That's why I didn't go to the airport with you," he said, giving her a crooked smile. "I told Paul to tell you I had taken the papers down to Lazards instead of him. I didn't want you to catch on. I wanted this to be a surprise."

She gave a cry. "Paul was upstairs?"

"Sure. I left him to finish things off."

She got to her feet unsteadily, holding on to a chair for support.

Emory smiled up at her, amused, mocking. "I got back to the house to get my bags and he was still there."

She stared at him wide-eyed, speechless, her face ashen.

"And he was there when I left," he added quietly.

A HABIT FOR THE VOYAGE   Robert Edmond Alter

THE MOMENT Krueger stepped aboard the steamer he was aware of a vague sense of something gone wrong. He had never understood the atavism behind these instinctive warnings, but he had had them before and usually he had been right.

He paused at the head of the gangplank, standing stock-still on the little bit of railed deck overlooking the after well deck. Down in the well, the Brazilian stevedores were just finishing with the last of the cargo. The steward was standing just inside a door marked *De Segunda Clase*, with Krueger's shabby suitcase in his hand. He looked back at Krueger with an air of incurious impatience.

Krueger took a last look around, saw nothing out of the ordinary, and stepped across the deck to follow the steward.

It came again—a last split-second premonition of danger —so sharply that he actually flinched. Then, as a black, blurred mass hurtled by his vision, he threw himself to one side, and the object, whatever it was, smacked the deck with an appalling crash, right at his feet.

He shot but one glance at it—a metal deck bucket filled to the brim with nuts and bolts and other nameless, greasy odds and ends. He moved again, stepping quickly to the right, rooting his hand under and around to the back of his raincoat to get at the snub-nosed pistol in his right hip-pocket, staring upward at the shadowy promenade deck just above him and at the railed edge of the boat deck above that.

He couldn't see anyone. Nothing moved up there.

The steward was coming back with a look of shocked disbelief.

"Nombre de Dios, señor! Qué pasa?"

Krueger realized that the stevedores were also watching him from below. He quickly withdrew his empty hand from under his coat.

"Some idiot almost killed me with that bucket! That's what happened!"

The steward stared at the loaded bucket wonderingly. "Those deckhands are careless dogs."

Krueger was getting back his breath. The steward was right; it had been an accident, of course.

Krueger was a linguist. He felt perfectly at home with seven languages; it was important in his business. He said, *"Lléveme usted a mi camarote."* The steward nodded and led him down a sickly lit corridor to his second class stateroom.

It was on the starboard and there wasn't much to it. A verdigris-crusted porthole, a sink on the right, a wardrobe on the left, and one uncomfortable-looking bunk. That was that.

Krueger gave the steward a moderate tip and sat down on the bunk with a sigh, as though prepared to relax and enjoy his voyage. He always maintained a calm, bland air in front of the serving class. Stewards, pursers, waiters and desk clerks had an annoying way of being able to recall certain little mannerisms about you when questioned later.

The steward said, *"Gracias, señor,"* and closed the door after himself. Krueger stayed where he was for a moment, then he got up and went over to bolt the door. But there was no bolt. He could see the holes where the screws had once been driven into the woodwork of the door, but the bolt had been removed.

That was the trouble with second-class travel. Nothing was ever in its entirety; nothing ever functioned properly. The bunks were lumpy, the hot-water tap ran lukewarm, the portholes always stuck. Krueger had had to put up with this nonsense all his life. The Party's rigorous belief that a penny saved was a penny earned was frequently an annoying pain in the neck to Krueger. Still—they were his best clients.

He took a paper matchbook from his pocket and wedged it under the door. It just did the trick. He opened his case and got out a roll of adhesive tape, cut four eight-inch strips, then got down on his knees and placed his pistol up underneath the sink and taped it there. Second-class stewards also had a bad habit of going through your things when you were out of your compartment.

He never relied upon a firearm for his work. It was messy and much too obvious. He was a man who arranged innocent-looking accidents. The pistol was purely a weapon of self-defense, in case there was a hitch and he had to fight his way out, which had happened more than once in his checkered career.

He was fifty-three, balding, inclined to be stout, and had a face as bland as a third-rate stockbroker's, unless you looked close at his eyes, which he seldom allowed anyone to do. He had worked at his trade for thirty years. He was an assassin.

He sat back in his bunk and thought about the man he was going to kill aboard this ship.

Unconsciously his right hand went up to his ear and he began to tug at the lobe gently. Catching himself at it, he hurriedly snatched his hand away. That was a bad habit with him, one that he had to watch. They were dangerous in his line of work, bad habits, exceedingly dangerous. They pinpointed you, gave you away, gave an enemy agent a chance to spot you. It was like walking around in public wearing a sign reading: *I Am Krueger, the Assassin!*

He remembered only too vividly what had happened to his old friend Delchev. *He* had unconsciously developed a bad habit—the simple, involuntary gesture of tugging his tieknot and collar away from his Adam's apple with his forefinger. Through the years the word had gotten around; the habit had been noted and renoted. It went into all the dossiers on Delchev in all of the world's many secret-service files. He was earmarked by his habit. No matter what alias or disguise or cover he adopted, sooner or later his habit gave him away. And they had nailed him in the end.

Krueger had known of another agent who used to break cigarettes in half, and still another who picked his ear, always the same ear. Both dead now—by arranged accidents.

And there was one colorful fellow who went by so many aliases that he was simply referred to by those in the business as Mister M. Krueger had always felt that he could have tracked M down within six months, had someone offered to make it worth his while. Because there was a notation in the dossiers on M of a bad habit that simply screamed for attention. M always tabbed himself by marking paper matchbooks with his thumbnail, orderly-spaced little indentations all up and down the four edges.

Well, at least tugging your earlobe wasn't that bad. But it was bad enough and Krueger knew it. He must be more attentive to his idiosyncrasies in the future. He had to weed all mannerisms out of his character until he became as bland as a mud wall.

The distant clang of a ship's bell reached him. The deck began to vibrate. Then the engines went astern with a rattle that he felt up his spine. A pause and then the engines went ahead, throbbing peacefully.

All right. Time to go to work. Time to view the future victim.

The dining room adjoined the saloon and they were both very dingy affairs. Cramped, too. And you could see rust streaks down the white walls at the corners of the windows. It all added up to greasy, overseasoned, poorly prepared food. But Krueger remained calm and benign; never call attention to yourself by being a complainer.

He sandwiched himself between a fat lady and a Latin priest, picked up his napkin and started to tuck it in his collar, but caught himself in time and put in on his lap instead.

Watch it; watch that sort of thing. You were the napkin-in-the-collar type on the last assignment. Never repeat the same mannerisms! He smiled at the man across the table, saying, "Pass the menu if you will, please."

The man addressed was an ineffectual-looking little fellow of about forty, with thinning hair and spectacles. His name was Amos Bicker and he was slated for a fatal accident —arranged by Krueger.

Krueger studied him surreptitiously. He certainly didn't look like the sort who needed killing. He had that civil-service-employee aspect. However, some way or another, innocent or not, he must have placed himself in this position of jeopardy by getting in the Party's path. Krueger's instructions had called for Immediate Elimination. So be it. Now for the means. . . .

He caught his hand halfway to his ear. *Dammit!* He carried the gesture through, switching its course to scratch the back of his neck. Then he studied the menu. Two of his favorites were there: oyster cocktail and New York cut. He ordered them, then turned to the priest, trying him first in Spanish, which worked. Actually he was thinking about the man across the table, Bicker, and the permanent removal of same.

Krueger always favored obvious accidents. So, when aboard ships, man overboard. This could be handled in a variety of ways. One, make friends with the victim, suggest a late stroll along the promenade deck; then a quick judo blow and. . . . Two, again make friends and (if the victim were a drinking man) drink him under the table, and then. . . . Or three, (and this method had great appeal to Krueger, because it eliminated public observance of his contact with the victim) slip into the victim's room in the wee hours of the morning, and jab him with a small syringe which induced quick and total unconsciousness, and after that . . . well, what followed was simple enough. Man overboard.

The steward brought Krueger his oyster cocktail. Krueger reached for his small fork and gave a start. Something was rubbing his left leg under the table. He leaned back in his chair and raised the cloth. A mangy-looking old cat—ship's cat, probably—was busy stropping himself against Krueger's thick leg.

"Kitty, kitty," Krueger said. He loved animals. Had he led a more sedentary life, he would have had a home, and the home would have been filled with pets. And a wife too, of course.

A minor ship's officer appeared in the starboard doorway. *"Dónde está Señor Werfel?"* he asked at large.

"Here!" Krueger called. That was one thing he never slipped on; he could pick up and drop an alias like the snap of the fingers.

"The captain wishes to see you for a moment, *señor.*"

A multitude of *why's* came clamoring alive in Krueger's brain. Then he caught the obvious answer and stood up, smiling. That accident with the bucket. It was annoying because the incident called undue attention to him—the steward, the stevedores, this officer, all the passengers, and now the captain.

He met the captain on the starboard wing of the flying bridge. The captain, originally some conglomeration of Mediterranean blood, was profuse in his apologies regarding the accident. Krueger laughed it off. It was nothing, truly. Those things happened. He wished the captain would put it out of his mind, really. He shook the captain's hand, he accepted the captain's cigar. He even allowed the captain to allow him to inspect the bridge.

He returned to the dining room wearing his professional bland smile. But something had happened during his absence.

The passengers were against the walls. The cook and his

assistants and the steward formed a more central ring. But the star of the scene was on the floor in the exact center of the room. It was the ship's cat and it was stretched out to an incredible length and going through the most grotesque mouth-foaming convulsions.

"*Ohh,* Mr. *Wer*fel!" the fat lady who had been seated next to Krueger cried. "I did a *ter*rible thing! No! Come to think of it, it was *for*tunate that I did! Certainly fortunate for *you!*"

"What?" Krueger said sharply, his eyes fixed on the convulsed cat. "What did you do?"

"That *poor* little dear jumped up on your seat after you left. He wanted your oysters! Of course I held him off, but you were so long in returning, and there are so many flies in here, you know."

"You gave him my oysters," Krueger said.

"Yes! I finally did! And before any of us knew it, the poor little thing went into those *awful* . . . "

"I'd better put the poor thing out of its misery," the priest said, coming forward. No one offered to help him.

Krueger stalled for an interval, until the passengers had thinned out, then he led the steward aside. "What was wrong with those oysters?" he demanded.

The steward seemed utterly flabbergasted. "*Señor,* I don't know! Ptomaine, you think? They were canned, of course."

"Let's see the can," Krueger said.

There was a faint scent of taint to the can—if held close to a sensitive nose. Krueger put it down and looked at the steward.

"Anyone else order oysters?"

"No, *señor.* Only yourself."

Krueger forced up a smile. "Well, accidents will happen." But he certainly wished there were some way he could have had that can, more especially the dead cat, analyzed. He returned to his stateroom more angry than shaken.

Well, that had been close. Too close. Look at it either way you wanted to, he had been a very lucky man. Of course, it *could* have been ptomaine . . . those things happened, . . . but when you coupled it with the business about the bucket. . . .

He went over to the sink and reached under for his gun. It wasn't there. The tape was there, neatly, but not the gun.

Now wait, he warned himself, pulling at his earlobe. A sailor could have kicked over the bucket by accident. Bolts are frequently missing from doors in rumdum ships like this. Ptomaine does occur in carelessly canned meats. And stewards do rifle compartments.

But the combination still spelled suspicion. Yet, supposing his suspicions were right, what could he do about it? He couldn't disprove that the bucket and food poisoning were accidents; and if questioned about the missing pistol, the steward would appear to be the epitome of innocence.

I must tread carefully, he thought. Very, very carefully, until this business is over. It's just possible that the Party slipped up somewhere on this assignment. Or was it possible that the Party. . . .

No! That was absurd. He had always given them faithful service; they *knew* that. And they knew, too, that he was one of the best in the business. No. No. Tugging furiously at his ear. Absurd.

He replaced the matchfolder under the door and, not satisfied with that, put his suitcase before it, flat, and, using the adhesive tape again, taped it to the deck. A man could get in, yes, but he would make a lot of noise doing it. He turned out the light and undressed and got into his bunk.

At first he thought it must be the wool blanket scratching him. Then he remembered that he had a sheet between his body and the blanket. Then he was really sure that it wasn't the blanket, because it moved when he didn't!

He felt the soft rasp of straggly fuzz across his bare belly, crawling sluggishly under the weight of the blanket, as a thing gorged with food. He started to raise the upper edge of the blanket and the thing, whatever it was, scrabbled anxiously toward his navel. He froze, sucking his breath, scared to move a muscle.

It stopped, too, as if waiting for the man to make the first decisive move. He could feel it on his naked stomach, squatting there, poised expectantly. It was alive, whatever it was, . . . it started moving again, he could feel the tiny feet (many of them) scuttling up toward his ribcage, the dry hairy fat little legs tickling his goose-fleshed skin, which rippled with loathsome revulsion.

He'd had it. With movements perfectly coordinated out of pure terror, he threw the blanket and sheet aside with his left and took a sweeping thrust across his stomach with his right forearm—as he rolled from the bunk to the deck.

He was up instantly and frantically fumbling for the light switch.

The thing scurried across the white desert of the bottom sheet—a thick-legged tarantula species, hideous, its furry body as fat as a bird's. Krueger snatched up a shoe and beat the thing over and over, and because of the give of the mattress the spider died the long, slow, frenziedly wiggly way.

Krueger threw the shoe aside and went to the sink to wash the clammy sweat from his face.

There was no call-button in the stateroom. He unbarricaded his door and shouted, *"Camarero!"*

A few minutes later the steward looked in with a sleepy smile. *"Sí, señor? Qué desea usted?"*

Krueger pointed at the crushed spider on his bed. The steward came over and looked at it. He made a face and grunted. He didn't seem overly surprised.

"Sí, it happens. It is the cargo, *señor.* The bananas. They come aboard in the fruit. Some of these *diablos* find their way amidships."

It was the kind of answer Krueger had expected, a reasonable explanation that left no room for argument. But it was getting to be too much. The tarantula was the last straw. He took his hand away from his earlobe and started getting into his clothes.

"Quisiera hablar con el capitán," he said flatly.

The steward shrugged fatalistically. If the unreasonable

gringo wanted to bother the captain at this time of night, it was none of his concern.

Krueger shoved by the steward rudely, saying, "I won't need you to find him. You're about as much help as a third leg." He was starting to forget all of his rules.

The captain was no help at all. He repeated all of the old sad-apple excuses: clumsy seamen, careless canning, the bothersome little hazards of shipping on a cargo steamer hauling bananas. . . .

"Now look here, Captain," Krueger said, angrily pulling at his ear. "I'm a reasonable man and I'll go along with everyday accidents, as long as they stay within the limits of probability. But all of these accidents have happened to *me*. Within one day."

"What is it that you're trying to say, Mr. Werfel? Surely you're not implying that someone aboard this ship is trying to kill you, are you? You don't have enemies, do you?"

Krueger balked at that. It was a subject that he wanted to stay away from. To get into it would be wading into a thick sea of endless, embarrassing explanations. He hedged.

"I said no such thing, Captain. All I'm saying is that these things keep happening to me aboard your ship, and I expect you to protect me from them."

"Certainly, Mr. Werfel. Let me see . . . yes! I can give you your choice of any of my officers' cabins. My own included. I can even assign a competent man to stay by your—"

"No, no, no!" Krueger said hastily. "That isn't at all necessary, Captain. I don't intend to act like a prisoner aboard this ship. Just assign me to a new cabin, one with a lock and bolt on the door."

Leaving the navigation deck, Krueger decided that he needed a drink. He would go down and see if the saloon was still open. His nerves were getting out of hand, and no wonder! The whole game was going very badly, turning sour on him. He was breaking all his time-tested rules, calling more attention to himself than a brass band.

He paused on the companionway overlooking the dark,

gusty boat deck. Someone was down there on the deck, someone familiar, leaning at the rail just to the stern of Number One starboard lifeboat.

Krueger took a quick swipe at his face, wiping away the tiny, moist needle-fingers of the sea mist, and came down another step . . . but quietly, ever so quietly. The man on the boat deck was Amos Bicker. He was mooning out at the black rambling sea, his forearms cocked up on the damp rail, his thin back to Krueger.

Krueger came down another quiet step, his narrowed eyes quickly checking out the points of professional interest.

Bicker had taken a position just inside the aft boat davit, to stand in the sheltering lee of the lifeboat's stern. He was leaning about a yard from the extreme corner of the rail; beyond that was nothing. There weren't even guard-chains, only the vacant space through which the davits swung the lifeboat. Below was the open sea.

Made to order. Krueger could finish the business here and now. Then he could concentrate all his wits on his own survival, guard himself against those recurring accidents . . . if that's what they were.

He came down the last step and put both feet on the boat deck.

Krueger and the victim were quite alone in the whispering sea-running night. And the unsuspecting victim thought that he was all alone. It wouldn't take much; just a sudden short rush and a bit of a push, catching Bicker on his side, and propelling him sideways right out into that empty waiting space.

Grinning tightly, Krueger broke into a cat-footed, avid rush.

All the lifeboats had returned and the captain had received their reports. Shaking his head, he reentered his office and went behind his desk and resumed his seat.

"Well," he said, "this is certainly a sorry business. Unfortunate that you had to be subjected to it, Mr. Bicker."

Amos Bicker was sitting hunched and drawn in his chair

facing the desk. The first mate had given him a shot of whisky but it didn't seem to be doing him much good. He was obviously in a bad state of nerves. His hands trembled, his voice too.

"You didn't recover the—uh—"

"Not a sign," the captain said. "Must have gone down like a stone. But please, Mr. Bicker, please do not let it prey upon you. You couldn't have done more than you did. You cried *man overboard* the moment it happened, and you even had the presence of mind to throw over a life-ring. You behaved admirably."

Mr. Bicker shivered and wrapped both hands about the empty shot glass. It was just possible, the captain thought, that he was going into shock. "Have a smoke, Mr. Bicker," he offered solicitously, passing over a cigarette box and matches.

Mr. Bicker had trouble lighting up, his hands shook so.

"He must have been mad—deranged," he said finally, hoarsely. "I didn't know the man, had never seen him, except in the dining room this evening. I was just standing there at the rail minding my own business, watching the sea without a thought in my head, and—and then I heard a—a movement, a sort of quiet rushing motion, and I looked around and there he was. Coming right at me! And the look on his face!"

"Yes, yes, Mr. Bicker," the captain said sympathetically, "we quite understand. There's no doubt in anyone's mind that there was something—well, odd, in Mr. Werfel's behavior. I have reason to believe that the poor devil actually thought that someone aboard this ship was trying to kill him. Mental delusion. Lucky for you that you reacted by stepping backwards instead of sideways or he might have taken you over with him."

Mr. Bicker nodded, staring at the carpets. One of his thumbnails absentmindedly was making orderly-spaced little indentations down one edge of the captain's paper matchbook.

THE EMPTY ROOM Donald Honig

THE GATE SQUEAKED with a soft feminine whine as he pushed it shut behind him. It made him pause for a moment on the walk and look at the house. The house was dark, rising somberly in the night. He wondered if she were awake, if perhaps the gate squeak had awakened her. But he really didn't care. It had gone so far now that he no longer cared. But the scenes were getting on his nerves, the constant repetitions, the accusations (which he no longer bothered to deny), the tirades.

He went up the walk and up the porch steps, reaching for his key. He let himself in, closing the door behind him. The moment he was in the house he sensed the hostility, the hatred generated there by her presence, by her constant unremitting resentment.

He slipped the key back into his pocket and was about to go upstairs when her voice came out of the dark, calm, controlled, pronouncing his name as if she had just decided what it was after hours of silent contemplation.

"Carl."

He stopped short at the foot of the stairs, his hand on the end of the bannister. He knew just where she was standing, beside the old grandfather clock in the corner near the door. When she waited for him it was always there.

"I should be used to it by now," he said, "but still you always startle me. Why the devil don't you let me know you're there? At least leave a light on."

"Why should I?" she said tersely from the dark, and he could see, without really looking, her sharp, tight-lipped face, her small intense eyes beginning to smolder. "Do you ever do anything in the light? Do you ever warn me?"

"You know where I was," he said, his voice quiet, patient. He could see her there now next to the clock, next to the momentous sway of the pendulum.

"No, I don't. I want you to tell me. I want you to keep telling me every time you go, until your conscience begins to throb against your head."

"Please, Laura. Not again."

"Yes again. And again and again a thousand times until you stop it."

"Or until I leave you."

"You'll never do that."

Now she would say: Because what will you do? Where will you go? You don't have money or a job. I'm keeping you here and supporting you with the money you married me for, doing it because once I believed in you and loved you. . . .

"Shut up!" he cried, even before she had said it.

"Yes, Carl."

"Dammit, Laura, can't you get used to a thing being what it is?"

"I'm used to you, Carl, but not what you're doing. No woman can ever accustom herself to that."

"Don't you know how many men see other women?"

"Are you trying to justify yourself, Carl?"

"I don't have to justify myself. Not to you or anyone else," he said. He began to feel a dangerous calm, the first broodings of a great storm. He began to turn cold. He could feel it rising in him, seeping into him from the tense,

hostile dark as from some black reservoir. He was fasci-
nated by it, as if it were new strength.

Who did she think she was? Did she think she owned
him body and soul with her rotten money?

He moved toward her, dizzily exhilarated by the strange,
dangerous calm that had seized him, the gray, heatless rage
that had begun to foam in his blood.

She was alarmed. The way he was moving towards her
through the dark: so silent, so intent.

"Carl!" she said, her voice oddly quiet, but sharp and
alive with terror. "Don't. . . ."

They struggled in the dark, against the clock. They
thudded against the old clock. The pendulum continued its
patient, momentous sway. They twisted away from the
clock, in tense, desperate quiet, her throat gargling hol-
lowly. He whirled her again and she fell to her knees, his
hands deep in her throat. She glared up at him, her mouth
gaping, wordless. Their eyes were mere inches apart; his,
cold, intent; hers, shining with death's light.

Then he let go. She fell sideways, heavily, inert. She lay
beneath the pendulum's infinite, dispassionate sway. From
deep in the old clock came a soft ticking, like a tongue
clucking remorse.

He looked around. It was odd, he thought, how nothing
had been disturbed, how the quiet was still there, how
everything was either naively unaware or disinterested. A
murder had just been committed here and nothing had
changed. Not even himself. He felt very calm about it. He
was not even breathing heavily. His hands, which had so
personally and effectively done it, felt no different. He was
standing there as if nothing had happened.

Well, perhaps nothing had. From the point of view of
punishment, murders occurred only if people found out
about them. Now, he wasn't going to go around and tell
people he had murdered his wife; nor would she be telling
anyone about it; and the only thing the old clock would
ever tell would be time.

He went into the living room, pulled closed the blinds

and turned on the lamp. He took off his jacket and lighted
a cigarette. From his easy chair in the living room he could
see part of Laura's crumpled body. Profoundly, he contemplated it, holding his cigarette in front of his mouth,
the smoke rising diagonally across his face. What to do
with her now?

Then he remembered reading recently about a skeleton
being dug out of the basement of some old house that was
being torn down. The skeleton—it had been that of a
woman—had been there for at least fifty years, it was es-
timated. There, he told himself, someone else had done it
and got by with it, lived his life and been buried a virtuous
man.

So Carl Bogan went down to the basement. With a pick-
axe he was able to split the floor. He tore up large chunks
of the concrete. Then he was digging in the dark, soft earth.
He trembled with excitement. Carefully he hollowed out a
place. Then—it was in the silent morning hours now—he
went upstairs and got his wife. He carried her down to the
cellar and placed her in the grave.

There was an old bag of cement in the cellar. It was the
sort that was already blended with sand, for the conve-
nience of the weekend handyman. He mixed the cement
with water and soon had healed over the wound in the floor.
By this time sunlight was streaming pleasantly through the
small cellar windows.

When he was through, he sat down in an old wicker
chair that was in the cellar and smoked a cigarette, staring
at the sinister place. Later he covered it with the hall rug

And so she was gone.

But so people would notice that. Now he set about contriv-
ing a story to account for her disappearance. That would
not be so difficult, though, because Laura had never made
herself very prominent in the neighborhood. It was not
one of those neighborhoods where each family knows the
pedigree and income of the next. Carl's philandering had
made Laura ashamed (she believed that everyone knew;
but Carl had been much smoother than that) and so she

had isolated herself to the extent where her sudden absence would go unnoticed.

To her distant relatives in California, he wrote that she was ill. He took care not to alarm them, for he did not want them suddenly rushing to visit. (Laura was a fairly wealthy relative.) But he made his point. In fact, that afternoon he wrote four different letters to the relatives, to be mailed out a week apart, describing Laura's various sufferings, improvements, relapses, and subsequent death.

A few days passed. On the third day he realized he had not left the house since the night of the murder. He chided himself. There was nothing to fear, no one would rush in and dig her up if he left. But that was the feeling he had.

Then the telephone rang. He picked it up. The call was for Laura. It was the butcher. Mrs. Bogan had not come by for her order. Was there anything wrong?

"No," Carl said. "Nothing is wrong. Mrs. Bogan isn't feeling well."

Sympathy from the butcher. Just the thing he needed. He cut short the butcher and hung up.

It started him thinking again. He had said there was nothing wrong, then went on in the next breath and said that she was sick. Things like that could make people suspicious. Maybe the people in the neighborhood weren't that blind, that indifferent after all. Eventually someone would begin to notice that Mrs. Bogan was no longer there, would begin to ask questions.

Laura might have had some friends. Thinking about that, Carl realized that he knew very little about his wife's habits. He was out of the house for whole days, sometimes for several days. How did he know what she did, to whom she talked?

He took a nap that afternoon. During it he had a bad nightmare. As desperately as his subconscious struggled to break the bond of sleep and wake him, it could not. He slept, sweating and tossing, through the long, harrowing nightmare. Laura was trying to dig her way out through the cellar. He could hear her scratching. There were muffled cries of terror and rage. The scratching grew louder, became a pounding. The concrete began to buckle. There was a terrible eruption in the cellar, rocking the foundation, the walls, rattling the windows.

He sprang up, his eyes aghast at what they had just seen. He looked around. It was very quiet. Too quiet. He sensed some deception. In his stockinged feet he ran down to the basement, his heart flooded with dread. In his panicky haste he almost tripped going down the cellar steps. Then he was there, standing over the rug, hot with apprehension. He bent and using both hands snatched it back.

The spot was undisturbed. He laid the rug back in place and stood up straight. He covered his eyes with his hand. What was the matter with him? Then he knew. He had been asking for such a nightmare, hanging around the house like that.

So he went out. Immediately he felt refreshed, relieved, as if some dark challenge had been withdrawn. He stood on the sidewalk in front of the house, in the bright sunlight. Then a voice said:

"Why, Mr. Bogan."

Immediately his heart constricted, the serpent of conscience binding it. He mustered his composure, rebuking himself for having to muster it.

The woman next door was standing there, a rather fat woman in blue jeans and one of her husband's abandoned white shirts. She held a pair of hedgeclippers in her hand.

"How are you, Mr. Bogan?"

He was fine.

"And Mrs. Bogan? I haven't seen her for almost a week now."

There! Gone only three days and already it was almost a week. Next they would begin whispering. Then they would accuse him of murder.

"She's not feeling well."

A lisp of sympathy. As if this woman really cared! Blasted busybody. Next she would want to know—

"Is there anything I can do?"

"No, no thank you."

"Is she very ill?"

"I don't know."

"Have you had the doctor?"

Already in the woman's eyes was the accusation, not of murder yet (give them time!), but that he had beat her; that she was laid up with bruises.

"Yes. He says she needs rest. Rest and absolute quiet."

"May I drop in on her? Perhaps I can cook her some soup."

"No, no thank you," he said quickly. Too quickly. Damn, what was the matter with him! Then: "I'm taking care of her."

"But when you're off at work. . . . " They still believed he worked. At least he had kept *that* from them. But this fool woman was persistent. She would remain persistent until she became suspicious. And all out of the goodness of her heart.

"I'm going to take in a nurse," he said. He said that too quickly. But he had to say it.

The woman smiled. Not suspicious now, not even persistent. It was remarkable what a small lie could do, in the right place. He smiled. They smiled at each other, in the sunlight.

Then he went back into the house, locking the door. He sat down. What had he said? But it had been the only way to drive her back. A woman like that could become possessed by her good intentions and invade the house with her soup.

But maybe it wasn't such a bad idea after all. He began to think seriously about it. While he couldn't very well hire a nurse, he *could* bring in someone to take care of the house, someone to cook and clean while his wife went through her illness. The person needn't ever have to see Mrs. Bogan. Mrs. Bogan would be deathly ill. She would require absolute rest and quiet. There would be strict orders about that. That would alleviate all suspicion. It would give him breathing time while he pondered what to do. But either way, he had committed himself to getting someone.

An ad went into the paper. Someone needed to keep a house while the mistress was ill. Someone to cook and clean and mind her business.

A few days later Betta Cool rang the bell. Carl opened the door. She was holding the newspaper, the page folded to the want ads. She was a tall woman with a rather pale face, not pretty, but not homely either. Pale and almost pretty, with thin, fine lips and clear, thoughtful eyes. Not yet forty, his expert eye told him. And a woman, his finely honed instincts in these matters told him, who might even be trusted, eventually. Anyhow, a woman who would not talk. He could tell that she was already replete with other secrets.

There was a quiet, thoughtful interview. Mrs. Cool—divorced, she said—had done this sort of thing before. She lived on the other side of town, alone. She answered his questions with monosyllables, having about her a rather English, or perhaps it was Irish, way.

Cook?

"Yes."

Keep house?

"Yes." And she volunteered: "I can nurse, too, if I should be asked."

"Oh, no," Carl said. "This is strictly a domestic job. Mrs. Bogan needs absolute rest and quiet, that's all she needs." He said this in the gravest of whispers, to emphasize. "The doctor looks in on her once a week."

Mrs. Cool gave him a long, steady gaze. She wanted to know something, but would not ask her question directly.

So he told her, slowing his voice with the proper emotion, "She was to have a child."

Mrs. Cool sympathized.

"She's very, very weak," Carl said, lowering his eyes in despair, trying to make it as ominous as he could without abandoning all hope.

So the pact was made. Mrs. Cool would come in the

mornings and clean the house—downstairs only—and cook Mrs. Bogan's meals. Mr. Bogan would take them upstairs —where he would sit in Laura's room and eat them and bring the empty dishes back down with Mrs. Bogan's comments.

"You're a fine cook, she says, Mrs. Cool."

"Thank you, sir."

He watched her. Not a bad-looking woman, either. And occasionally she stole a glance at him. She was feeling terribly sorry for him, he sensed. He knew what that could lead to. Women and their pity. She prepared special meals for him, with which he was forced to stuff himself.

So it became a routine. It went on for a week, then two weeks. Every morning and afternoon Carl dutifully and solemnly carried the cloth-covered trays up to the empty room, closed the door and sat there and ate, occasionally murmuring a few words of conversation, hoping Mrs. Cool downstairs would hear.

Every afternoon at four she departed. One afternoon he walked her to the bus stop.

"How is she getting on?" Mrs. Cool asked.

He shook his head. "She stays the same. And that's not good. The doctor said—he was here yesterday just after you left—that she's not making any progress, and in her condition that's bad. She just lies there, staring at the walls, hardly saying a word."

"Thinking of the child, no doubt."

"Most likely."

They came to the bus stop. She looked at him. "Frankly, Mr. Bogan," she said, "what do you think her chances are?"

"Between you and me, Mrs. Cool, they aren't good. I could tell by the doctor's eyes."

"You poor man. How awful for you. I know that kind of loneliness. I have it in my own life."

"Do you?"

"Yes."

This next he could not repress: "Perhaps we might give one another some cheering."

He expected no response. But she surprised him.

"Perhaps some evening a neighbor can sit with her and we can see a movie together. It might do you some good."

"Yes," he said, brightening. "I wouldn't be surprised that it might."

So a "neighbor" began coming in the evenings. And Carl Bogan was at it again with a woman. Mrs. Cool's loneliness, her aloofness, once penetrated, crumbled with a devastating crash.

Their evenings were gay and pleasant. He hardly seemed a man with a dying wife. They danced and went to shows and drank, and he took her home.

"You make me feel like a schoolgirl all over again, Carl," Betta said.

"I think we both needed a change."

"You don't think what we're doing is wrong, do you?"

"Of course not. And get that idea out of your head, Betta. We're simply two human beings trying to make the best out of the poor lot that life's given us."

"How soon do you think it will be for her?" Betta asked.

"I don't know," he said. "She never changes. She just lies there."

"It seems interminable."

Which was exactly how Carl wanted it to be. He had begun to wonder what he ought to do. He could have Laura die, of course. But that would present new problems. The burial could hardly be secret. People would have to be informed. A death certificate would have to be made out. And there was the undertaker. All sorts of complications, and this would be the case even with a private funeral.

He even thought of taking Betta into his confidence. She loved him. That made a woman a slave. But he was afraid. He had got by with it this far and did not like the idea of jeopardizing himself. But still, something would have to be done, and soon.

Probably the only thing he could do was disappear. And that wasn't as bad as it sounded. There was an excellent chance that Laura too, like the other woman, would not be found for fifty years. He could say he was taking her away to convalesce. That would be the end of it. Who would ever think of digging up the basement?

He was pondering all of this as he brought Laura's tray up to her. He sat in the room and ate, staring out the window. He could sell the house. At least he would have some money from that. Of course it was a pity to lose all the rest of Laura's money, but that was the penalty he had to pay.

And then a new idea struck him. Why lose all of that money? Why not Betta in place of Laura? With a private funeral he could get away with it. The only ones who would see her would be the undertakers, and they did not know Laura. It was a veritable stroke of genius. How wonderfully and ironically the pieces fell into place! But he would have to figure it carefully.

He came down to the kitchen with the empty dishes.

"Did she eat well?" Betta asked.

"Yes," he said, looking at her strangely.

"Carl," she said. "Do you love me?"

"Why, Betta, I think you know that. In fact I've been upstairs thinking about you."

"When she's gone, will you still love me?"

"More than ever."

"Then it will be soon, Carl."

"What do you mean?"

She looked at the empty dishes. Then she looked at him.

"I put enough poison in her food to make it easy for her."

He blanched. Then he began to feel it, the massive feel of it clouding up through him.

He managed to call her a fool before he died, writhing furiously on the floor under her astonished eyes.

I'LL GO WITH YOU   Hal Dresner

WITH AN AIR of nervous, impulsive decision, the little man in the gray suit crossed the club car, drink in hand, and stood before Lowe.

"Mind a little company?" he asked with a strained smile.

"Not at all," Lowe said. He regarded the man—fortyish, balding, elfin-featured—as he moved his newspaper from the booth seat.

The little man sat down gratefully. "Can I buy you a drink?" he asked.

"No, thanks," Lowe smiled. "One's about my limit on trains."

"How about a ginger ale?"

"Okay. A ginger ale. Thanks."

The man ordered it and a Scotch for himself, finishing the drink he was holding in the time it took for the barman to bring the new ones. "You going far?" he asked when the attendant had left.

"Baltimore," Lowe said.

"That's where I get off, too. Baltimore." He paused, looked down at his drink, suddenly picked it up and drained it in a swallow. "Look," he said, "I know this must seem funny. I don't usually start conversations with strangers but I had to have someone to talk to."

"Train trips are boring," Lowe said.

"It's not that," the man said. "It's not that at all. Listen, do you mind if I talk about it? It wouldn't get you involved. It's only me they're after."

"Who?" Lowe said, slightly amused.

"The syndicate or whatever they call themselves. I don't know. It's so crazy that I'm mixed up in this at all. You know what I do for a living? I work in a Western Union office. I've worked there all my life, never held another job. I started as a delivery boy making ten dollars a week and worked my way up to office manager. Ninety-six dollars a week. Big deal. Does that sound like the kind of man to get involved with hoodlums?"

The question was obviously rhetorical.

"It's my brother," the man said. "My older brother. All my life I've always looked up to him. *He* was the smart one; *he* went to college; *he* started his own law practice. Fifteen, twenty, thirty thousand dollars a year he was making but it wasn't enough for him. Nothing was ever enough for him." He clasped his hands and stared down at them as if he were reading. "So somehow he got involved with the rackets. Maybe through one of his big-shot clients, I don't know. I didn't know anything about it until two weeks ago; he came to my apartment and told me they were after him. Something about these papers that he had been holding for them and then they wanted them back so he gave them back and then somehow they found out he had a copy of them." He shrugged helplessly. "He told me so much and so fast with all the legal terms that I hardly understood a word he was saying except that he wanted *me* to hold the papers. I didn't *want* to hold them. I told him take them somewhere else, put them in a vault, anywhere. Why should I want to get involved? What do I know about rackets? I'm a plain ordinary man. But no. He said they had to be in a safe place where he could get at them in a hurry. You'd think he'd given them to his wife? No. He didn't want *her* to know anything about it. For her, it was too complicated but me—his *brother*—that was different." His jaw tightened in an expression that was both vicious and impotent. He looked down at his empty glass and then over to Lowe's untouched ginger ale. "You sure you don't want a drink?" he asked.

"No, thanks."

"Well, I'm going to have another one." He signalled the barman. "I don't think I've had a dozen drinks in my whole life and now I feel like I've got to have one every minute. Cigarettes, too. I smoked so many in the last three days, I can't stand the taste of them anymore. I'm like an animal. I don't eat. I don't sleep. All I can—" He stopped as the barman approached and waited until the man had set down the drink and left.

"They killed him," he said quietly. "A week ago they killed my brother. They rang his bell at nine o'clock at night, he opened the door and they shot him six times with a machine gun." His hand tightened about the glass and his teeth bit into his lower lip until the flesh whitened.

"When I heard about it," he said in a carefully controlled voice, "I couldn't believe it. To gangsters those things happen but to your own brother? I walked around in shock for days. Then I remembered about the papers, and you know what I did?" He looked up, begging absolution. "Like a *fool*," he said vehemently, "you know what I did? I burned them! I just dropped them down the incinerator without even opening the envelope. I tell you, I was still in a daze. All I could think was that they had killed him because of the papers so I had to get rid of them. Like a fool, I thought that. Then, three days ago, they called me. 'You've got some papers that belong to us,' they said. I told them I didn't know anything about it. I told them they must have the wrong party and I hung up. The next night they called again. Then I told them I had burned the papers. I told them I hadn't even opened the envelope. I swore it to them. You know what they said to me? 'Find them,' they said. That's all, just 'Find them.'"

He picked up his drink and took a large swallow. When he set the glass down, he seemed to have aged another year. "You know I went down and looked in the incinerator?" he said. "I thought maybe the papers hadn't been burned yet, maybe they were still lying there."

"They weren't?" Lowe asked.

The man shook his head. "Ashes. That's all that was there. Ashes. And then last night they called again. 'By tomorrow night,' they said. They were coming over the next night to pick up the papers and I'd better have them." He took another swallow and looked at Lowe. "What would you do?" he asked pitifully. "Tell me, what would *you* do? Go to the police and if they believe you, they put a detective to sit in front of your door for a few nights? So then nothing happens and the detective leaves and then they kill me. Or maybe they get me one day when I'm going to work. Or coming home. I can't spend the rest of my life in my room. What would you do?" he asked plaintively.

"I don't know," Lowe said. "I imagine I'd do the same thing you're doing."

"I'm running away," the man said. "My mother still lives in Baltimore so that's where I'm going. It's the only place I can go. And if they know that from my brother, then I'm running right to them. For all I know they could be on the train with me this minute. What do I know about racketeers? I don't even know what they look like. If they don't look like the ones on television, I wouldn't recognize them if they came up and sat down beside me."

The barman came over with the check. He was a tall redhead with narrow features and a starched smile. "Anything else, gentlemen?" he asked.

The little man shook his head and put a bill on the table. "No change," he said.

The attendant thanked him and walked back to the bar.

"He could even be one of them," the man said pathetically.

"Maybe they decided to believe you and forget the whole thing," Lowe said.

"Maybe," the man said weakly. "And maybe I'll be dead in ten minutes, too." He finished his drink and pushed the glass from him. "I didn't mean to worry you about it," he said. "I just had to have somebody to talk to. If you're smart you'll forget all about it." He stood up, shakily. "Now I feel a little dizzy from the drinks. I think I'll go to the observation car to get some air. Goodbye," he said and started toward the door.

"Wait," Lowe said. "I'll go with you."

THE WATCHDOGS OF MOLICOTL Richard Curtis

WHEN LOU ROMER looked up from his drink he saw a familiar pair of eyes scrutinizing him from the other side of the horseshoe bar. Though the owner of the eyes wasn't hostile, Lou preferred not to get involved anyway. In his racket, to be recognized by friends was to be pinched by enemies sooner or later. Besides, Myron Tweemey was by no means his friend. He was merely on the same side of the law as Lou, and on that side there's no such thing as a friend.

Lou dropped twenty pesos on the counter and made for the door, but Tweemey got up too, escorted him into the cool evening air of Mexico City, and fell into pace with him. Lou steered for one of the darker streets paralleling La Reforma, the main drag. He didn't want to be seen with Tweemey on any brightly lit streets.

Silently they strode, Lou a head taller and much better-looking than his turtle-beaked, heavy-lidded companion who had almost to trot to keep up with him. Cruising cabs beckoned to the two men with promises of exciting nights; a pair of buxom, dark-haired girls minced by, giving them seductive looks and giggling as they passed.

"A man could have some good times here, huh, Lou?"

Lou ignored the small talk. "How did you find out where I was?"

Tweemey said, "Well, let's just say that we both employ the services of the same gentleman in disposing of certain properties. He told me you were in town."

"Damn him. If he can't keep his mouth shut . . . " Lou increased his pace as if hoping the little guy would eventually drop away from exhaustion, but Tweemey kept up with him. "I didn't know we had anything to say to each other, Tweemey," Lou said without looking at him.

"Maybe we do and maybe we don't. I just wanted to congratulate you on that jewel heist at the St. Regis. They had a picture of Edith Glayde in the papers the next day that was most unbecoming an actress. She looked roaring mad."

Lou's chin quivered but he showed no other reaction. "I don't know what you're talking about."

Tweemey's teeth glowed under a street lamp. "As long as I know what I'm talking about, it doesn't matter if you do or not." Tweemey went on in a confidential whisper, "Let's face it, the details of that job practically spelled out your name. And, of course, our mutual friend showed me a gem or two that confirmed it."

"Remind me to rub that boy."

"He's all right, don't worry. He was just acting in the line of business. And your secret's safe with me."

"Yeah? For what price?"

Tweemey stopped and looked at Lou with a whipped puppy expression. "A stoolie I'm not, Lou."

"So what do you want?"

Lou faced Tweemey with ill-disguised malice and distrust. "Well," answered Tweemey, "I've been examining a certain enterprise which looks very promising. It requires two people, with our talents. I'd like to lay it out for you, Lou. If you like it, we'll go fifty-fifty. If you don't, I'll go my way and you'll go yours. But believe me, you'll snap it up. It's a pushover."

"That's what you said about Guarantee Loan, remember? Your carelessness almost landed us in the pen. Uh-uh. The first time we worked together was the last. I told you then, and I'm telling you now."

"Lou, how many times do I have to tell you? It wasn't carelessness; it was a one in a million coincidence. The guard forgot his . . . "

"I don't care what the guard forgot. You'd have to guarantee me better odds than a million to one."

"You're on."

Lou looked at him skeptically, but Tweemey's gaze was steady and confident. Lou hesitated, then said, "Can we go somewhere private?"

Tweemey beamed and suggested his hotel room, but Lou wasn't taking any chances. Tweemey left it up to him, and Lou guided his companion to a bench in one of the many little parks that stud Mexico City. In the lush, cinnamon-smelling greenery, their voices were muted. Tweemey explained the setup, emphasizing important points by tugging intermittently on Lou's lapel.

"You've heard of Molicotl?"

"Mining town, tourist trap."

"More than that. It sets on top of a mountain that I'd swear is solid silver, gold, precious and semiprecious stones. It hauls up a small fortune in raw stuff every day, and it's been doing that since the town was founded *two hundred years ago*." He yanked three times on Lou's jacket to make his point. "It's second only to Taxco in production," he went on, "and, like Taxco, they have a bunch of artists and crafts-men who make jewelry and sell it to tourists. There are dozens of shops. Most of them sell junk, but one or two carry high-class merchandise."

"Sure. Half-carat turquoises set in German silver."

"You should live so long. They've got fat diamonds set in platinum. Emeralds, sapphires, rubies. A lot of uncut gems in vaults, easy stuff to push because it isn't tagged. I was there, I saw it myself. It isn't Tiffany quality, I'll admit that, but it's Woolworth quantity, which amounts to the same thing. There's more goods there than you can carry away, I guarantee."

"Go on," Lou said, showing a flicker of interest for the first time.

"The stuff is stored in safes in the shops every night." Tweemey's teeth gleamed violet in the light from a neon store front on the other side of the park. "I think those safes came over with Cortez. I open three like them for practice every morning before brushing my teeth."

"Do the owners live in the same place?"

"Only in the poorer shops, which we won't be hitting. As for the one we will be doing, the owners live in the rich section up in the hills."

"Guards, watchmen?"

Tweemey shook his head vigorously.

"Alarms?"

Tweemey laughed. "They're lucky to have any electricity at all. No alarms."

"Cops?"

"A fat constable and a deputy who's the town idiot. The jail is on the other side of town from the shops, and the narrow streets would make it impossible for them to get to us quickly—if the police had a car, which they don't. The constable and his deputy spell each other at the *juzgado* —that's where "hoosegow" comes from, y'know—so one or the other is always sleeping. The only thing is the dogs, but I'll get to them in a second."

Lou pulled Tweemey's fingers off his lapel. "Wait a minute. What dogs? What about them? You'll get to them now." He scanned the heavy-lidded eyes for signs of cupidity. If Tweemey was saving the dog bit, it must be the hitch and Lou would see it in the man's eyes. Yet Tweemey's face registered no reluctance to go into it. In fact, his grin broadened.

"Sure, Lou, sure. I just thought I'd save the funniest part for last. I got nothing to hide. Well," he said, "every shopkeeper has a mutt that's supposed to be a watchdog. And I'll say this for them: they bark at the slightest sound."

Lou had heard enough. He rose suddenly to his feet. "Nice seeing you again, Tweemey. Lots of luck in your enterprise. I can see you'll need a partner all right—to carry dog biscuit."

Tweemey jumped up. "Hold on, don't split until you've heard me out. I'm just trying to squeeze a little drama out of this bit." He fell back onto the bench and drew Lou by the hem of his jacket back down beside him. "Look, the dogs *do* bark at the slightest sound. But do you know what the slightest sound is in that town?"

Lou volunteered nothing and simply eyed Tweemey coolly, impatiently.

"The slightest sound is a dog barking!" He prodded Lou's lapel on each word. "Don't you see what I'm getting at? The hounds bark all night long. As soon as the sun goes down and one dog barks, the rest join in and it goes on like a chain reaction until the sun comes up next morning. You never heard such a racket in your life. They had to put the tourist joints way outside of town because nobody can sleep through all that noise, except the natives. These Mexicans—they do everything backwards."

Lou felt the knot in his stomach relax as he began to grasp what his friend was saying.

"So you see, Lou, what good is a watchdog that doesn't shut up? It's like a shepherd that cries 'wolf' every ten seconds. If the cops came running every time a watchdog barked in that town, it would look like a Mack Sennett movie all night long every night—except that there's not enough cops to stuff into a phone booth. So as far as I can see, the only function of these dogs is to make enough commotion to scare away prospective prowlers."

"But the dogs are vicious, aren't they?"

Tweemey's laughter shattered the peaceful stillness. "Lou, they are the scrawniest, mangiest cowards I've ever seen. They slink away if you *think* 'cat.' "

"Then what good are they?"

"Put it this way. If you were the average safecracker, would you enter a joint where the siren was already blowing? Of course not. That's the psychology of these Mexicans. But it's bum psychology to anyone with brains."

"And actually," Lou said, making the first contribution of the evening, "all that noise would work in our—to the advantage of anyone trying to get some work done late at night."

Tweemey's confident nod seemed to hammer the final nails into the foolproof case he was constructing. "Exactly. Now let me explain a few other things." Tweemey told him that the man behind this job was their mutual friend, the fence, Diaz. Diaz had suggested the job and paid for Tweemey's scouting trip down to Molicotl. When Tweemey had returned and reported the job a cinch, the fence put him on to Lou. "Diaz wouldn't tell me your whereabouts if he didn't see some percentage in it."

"What's the deal?"

"He'll pay for everything; the trip down, the getaway, and even tickets out of the country. We reciprocate by using his services in disposing of the ice. It costs us nothing, see, and we have a citizen helping us out at every step of the way. The night of the job one of Diaz's men will send a taxi to Molicotl. It'll take us to one of the small coast towns on the Pacific, and there'll be a launch. It'll carry us to Acapulco, where we meet Diaz, dump the stuff, and plane out for wherever we want to go." Tweemey slapped his knees as if he'd just concluded a perfect brief on a law case. "What do you say, Lou?"

Lou sat thoughtfully for several minutes, turning every side of the proposition over as if they were poker cards in a blind game. Lou's eyes shifted their focus from Tweemey's violet-lit turtle-face to the blue throbbing stars above the skyline of Mexico City. Finally he said "It sounds too easy."

"That's what I said, but after casing the thing for a week, I'm convinced there's no hitch. The people there simply think that between the town's partial isolation and the dogs' racket and the vaults, they're safe. The only real crime in that burg is shoplifting—by respectable tourists. I made a discreet inquiry, and the only attempt at something big in modern times was back in the twenties, when some

Chicago gentlemen made a daylight raid on three shops."

"What happened?"

"It worked. Or it would have, if they hadn't made a wrong turn on the road to Acapulco. They went over a cliff. We won't be taking that road," Tweemey said hastily.

Lou nodded, and after a long pause said, "You can count me in. But I want a look for myself."

"Fine, Lou. It'll be a pushover, take my word for it."

In the interests of not being seen together, they went down to Molicotl separately and took rooms in different hotels. They met guardedly in obscure places and were never seen together in La Joya Encantada, the shop they'd chosen to hit.

Lou covered just about every yard of the town on foot and sized up the shop from every conceivable angle. After five days of scrutiny, he came up with a clean bill of health. It looked as easy as Tweemey said it would be. Tweemey had been right about the dogs, too. They yapped and yammered all night long, and Molicotl at night was like a huge kennel before feeding time. The noise could drive a man crazy, and anyone with a faint heart would certainly think twice before raiding a shop guarded by one of these howling animals. But the dogs were all bark and no bite, and their racket would provide excellent cover for anyone entering and tinkering with a safe.

"Okay," Lou said to Myron Tweemey. "Tell Diaz to have a taxi here tomorrow night."

The next night, at the point where Molicotl's main street straightens out and aims westward to the sea, a black cab pulled inconspicuously onto a gravel shoulder. Lou and his companion, watching from a distance, saw the driver signal with a lighted cigarette. The two then proceeded down the steep, cobbled lanes towards El Centro, the plaza on which the town's most important civic and commercial buildings faced. Just off this square was Calle Naranja, the street on which La Joya Encantada stood. They drifted past the shop, their eyes peeled for dangerous circumstances. But they saw no one and heard nothing of note, so they reversed their direction and steathily made their way toward the shop. The sound of their heels was drowned completely in the clamor raised by the dogs. These dogs were meant to discourage and to frighten, and Lou had to admit to himself that they did their job. The ruckus was unnerving. It was all he could do to keep his reason on top of the irrational fear of being torn apart by a pack of mad, fang-snapping beasts.

The front of the shop was protected by a tall, steel accordion gate, which was stretched out and padlocked every evening at closing time. They could have worked the lock easily enough, but there was also a padlock on the front door behind the gate. This meant exposing themselves for too long on the main street while working on first one lock, then the other. They'd determined, therefore, that the side door, which faced a narrow alley, was far easier. It was a steel door with a lock built into the knob. Tweemey had it open in a few minutes. They ducked inside.

They were greeted by two yapping mongrels which sniffed them, lowered their heads and tails, and crept off under a workbench. Lou had been prepared to bash both animals, but the dogs were so laughably docile that he gave them no further thought.

Lou and Tweemey got down to business immediately, Tweemey hitting the vault in the workshop and Lou going to the one in a little alcove off the showroom. Tweemey's vault held the uncut gems and the gold, silver and platinum wire, while Lou's held the finished jewelry itself. Lou thought he got his safe open quickly, but when he heard the clicking of stones from Tweemey's side of the shop he realized Tweemey's educated fingers had beaten him by several minutes. When Lou's door swung open with a creak he saw a treasure of diamond, ruby, emerald and sapphire rings, bracelets and necklaces, plus jewelry of topaz, alexandrite and a host of other semiprecious stones. The craftsmanship was flawless and the designs were strikingly unusual.

He began sweeping the ice into his sack, and as he did he became aware of Tweemey's sibilant breathing, the creaking of floorboards, and the sound of his own heartbeat. It made him vaguely uncomfortable, but he couldn't understand why, for he was usually quite cool on a job and never let small sounds panic him. He tied his sack and stood up suddenly.

"Tweemey!" His whisper sliced through the silence.

"What's the matter? Some haul, huh?" Tweemey's whisper had the same jarring effect on him.

"Do you hear something?"

Tweemey met him in the center of the shop. "No."

"I don't either. Hey . . . " He became aware suddenly of a new sound, a sound from outside, a kind of shuffling noise. He recognized it as sandaled feet on cobblestones. Wavering orange light now came in through the shop windows. Lou ran to one of them and cautiously peered out.

Men with torches, clubs and rifles stood outside the door. Down the alley, men encircled another shop. Another band of Mexicans stood before the front of the shop, torches glowing and weapons, dark and mean-looking, in their hands. Sullen mobs stood in front of every building as far as he could see. Tweemey and Lou scurried all over the shop looking for a way out, but there were only the two doors. They were surrounded. Lou's heart pounded madly and his teeth clamped his lower lip.

They exchanged a long, futile look and Tweemey started whimpering. "How did they find out we're here?"

"They don't know we're here," Lou said. They just know that somewhere in this town a place has been broken into. They're going to stand there until we come out. If we don't come out, they'll come in after us at daybreak." He sighed despairingly. "I knew you'd louse this thing up somehow."

"It's so quiet, Lou," was all the little safecracker could manage to say. "Why is it so quiet?"

All at once Lou realized how quiet it really was—and why. "The dogs!"

"That's right," Tweemey said. "They've stopped barking."

"They're watchdogs in reverse," Lou murmured, collapsing against a display case.

He saw it clearly now. Everywhere else dogs are trained to keep silent except when prowlers are about; *then* they bark. But the people of Molicotl went one step further. They tried to discourage people from even *thinking* of prowling. So they trained their dogs to bark all night. If a stranger was foolish enough not to get the message, and to try breaking into a place, its watchdog stopped barking. Dogs in neighboring shops became aware of the silence next door and they fell quiet too until a hush would radiate from shop to shop, and the whole town would grow still. The townspeople, accustomed to the barking, would be alerted by the quiet.

It was like the joke about the Londoner who slept through the bonging of Big Ben every night for years, but on the night the bell broke down and failed to toll, he awoke with a start, crying, "What was that?"

The dogs, having failed to discourage them with their noise, had trapped them with their silence.

Lou and Tweemey looked at each other, then made their decision. The dogs' tails fluttered amiably as they watched the two men open the door and the torches surge forward to engulf them.

THE AFFAIR UPSTAIRS Helen Nielsen

MRS. EMILY PROCTOR had the nicest roses on Roxbury Avenue, and that was because she never allowed the gardener near them. Samuel, her husband, could—under careful direction—spade the earth at fertilizing time; but the hired Japanese was required to confine his activities to the small patch of front lawn and the hedges.

Mrs. Emily Proctor always tended the roses herself. There were many of them. The climbers started at the entrance to the driveway and extended the entire length of the white brick wall that stretched to the rear of the lot. The bushes were at the corners of the building, front and rear, and the rose trees were in the patio that filled in the L created by the architectural design of Roxbury Haven, a ten-unit stucco, singles and doubles by lease only. Emily and Samuel Proctor resided in apartment 5A, the lower rear at the end of the patio where the small sign "Manager" was affixed to the door.

All of the lower apartments opened into the patio, and all of the upper apartments had small balconies with neat wrought-iron railings in front of sliding glass doors. From the rose trees in the patio, and from the corner bushes at the entrance and at the approach to the garage area, and from the climbers on the wall, Mrs. Emily Proctor, attired in smock, gardening gloves and straw coolie hat, had visual command of every doorway, every garage stall, and every person who entered or left Roxbury Haven. There was nothing about any tenant that she didn't know.

Mrs. Emily Proctor was happy.

On the day Haynes *versus* Haynes made its initial appearance on Judge Carmichael's docket, Emily timed her activities carefully. She had been spraying the Mary Margaret McBride at the entrance to the driveway for nearly thirty minutes, when Tod Haynes returned. She saw the black convertible come slowly down the street—very slowly for Tod Haynes, who was usually fast about everything. Fast, she mused darkly, in every way. The car was barely moving as it turned into the driveway, and his face, which she saw clearly before he saw her, was that of a man driving in his sleep—or one who had just been hit by a falling wall. And then a disturbing thing occurred. Tod Haynes saw Emily. He looked at her, glared at her; and then the convertible leaped forward, swerving slightly so as to force her back against the rosebush, and roared past on its way to the garage.

"Oh," Emily gasped. "That man!"

She didn't expect the Mary Margaret McBride to answer. The voice came as a surprise.

"Now, what's got into him? Is he drunk?"

"I wouldn't be surprised," Emily answered. "He drinks like a fish."

And then she remembered herself. Turning, she saw Mr. Kiley, the postman, who had just crossed the lawn and was arriving, mail in hand. Automatically, Emily reached up to brush back her hair and straighten the coolie hat.

"Oh, good morning, Mr. Kiley," she said. Her voice softened. "Now, I shouldn't have said that about Mr. Haynes. He's been having so much trouble."

"Sickness?" Kiley asked.

"Worse trouble than that, I'm afraid. Poor Mr. Haynes was sued for divorce by Mrs. Haynes only this morning."

Mr. Kiley shook his head sadly.

"Moral deterioration," he said. "There's a new series running in the evening paper that tells all about it, Mrs. Proctor. Homes breaking up. Children running wild. Moral deterioration. Gonna wreck the whole country."

And Emily Proctor smiled knowingly.

"You don't have to tell me!" she declared. "If you managed an apartment building, you wouldn't need to read the newspapers."

From where he stood, Mr. Kiley could see the row of balconies extending along the upper floor of the unit. Now, out of 4B, emerged Patti Parr—young, silver blonde, her lovely body still clad in a flimsy white negligée. She stretched luxuriously and stared up at the sky. Mr. Kiley watched appreciatively.

"I'll bet I wouldn't!" he said.

Emily glanced up at 4B, frowned and then reached for the mail in Mr. Kiley's hand. "Anything for me?" she asked brightly. "Oh, just another old bill! At least I can put the rest of it in the boxes for you. Lord knows, you're on your feet enough, Mr. Kiley! And I haven't another thing to do." By this time, Emily was nudging Mr. Kiley toward the sidewalk. "And I do hope you won't repeat anything I said about poor Mr. Haynes," she added. "If there's anything I can't stand, it's gossip."

Mr. Kiley moved on down the street, and Emily paused a moment to look after him. It was a lovely morning. The pre-school children were playing in the yards, and she wondered, idly, what these young mothers were thinking of to let their children leave such expensive toys scattered over the neighborhood, and why Mrs. Williams didn't do something about her daughter. The Williams child ate constantly and resembled a baby blimp.

When Emily turned back to the patio, she noted that Patti Parr had gone inside again. That was a relief. Her appearance had such bad timing. Tod Haynes would be returning from the garage at any moment. She went to the row of mailboxes and busied herself, listening without turning when the heavy footsteps came from the rear of the driveway. They came closer, and then stopped.

"Do you censor it for us, too?" Tod Haynes asked.

Emily, with most of the mail still in her hands, was trying pitifully to stuff old Miss Brady's *New Romances* into a mail slot designed for letters. When it dropped from her hands, Tod bent down quickly, retrieved it, and returned it to her. Her lips tried to form the words, "Thank you," but her voice didn't respond at all. Tod stared at her darkly and then stalked off toward the inside stairwell, leaving Emily Proctor with a peculiar feeling she would later recognize as the beginning of terror.

The marriage of Tod and Ann Haynes had disturbed Emily from the beginning. She was certain it would never last. Tod Haynes wasn't the husband type.

"Do you mean he doesn't look beat enough?" Sam asked. "Give him time."

It wasn't at all what Emily meant. Tod Haynes had a roving eye—any woman could see that—and Ann Haynes was nobody's fool. She was attractive in a self-assured way that Emily secretly envied. A businesswoman who assumed responsibilities and would expect a mate to do the same. Oh, Emily didn't guess or deduce all this. When apartments are as close as the apartments at Roxbury Haven; and when one of the legitimate duties of the co-manager is to inspect the units when they are vacated for new occupancy; and when—as it developed—such a situation occurred shortly after the Haynes moved into 5B, Emily couldn't avoid hearing one significant conversation which took place on the balcony one summer evening at dusk.

The magnolia tree Sam was always going to get trimmed grew up beside that balcony. Because of it, Emily, who was near the sliding doors inside 4B, heard when Tod and Ann stepped outside.

"Ouch!" Tod said. "So help me, someday I'll get an axe—"

Then Ann laughed softly, and there was one of those interesting silences when Emily's imagination made her feel slightly uncomfortable.

After a little while, Tod said, "No regrets, Mrs. Haynes?"

"No regrets," Ann answered. "What about you?"

"Oh, I'm getting used to the harness," Tod said. "I told you when I applied for the job—'experienced: no references.' "

"Tod—"

"—but a willingness to learn. Ann, this has to work."

"It will," Ann said.

"I mean, it *has* to. Life has to start making sense somewhere along the line."

By this time, Emily knew she was eavesdropping; but she always made herself believe that it was a part of her duty as manager to learn what kind of tenants she had. Credentials meant nothing. She could never see past anyone's teeth. And so she listened carefully as Tod Haynes continued.

"I blew it once," Tod said. "But I'm not going to blow it again. My luck changed the day I walked into Curtis's office and found you at the reception desk. Do you remember what you said to me?"

Ann's voice became professional.

"Mr. Curtis will see you in a few minutes, Mr. Haynes."

"No," Tod said. "I mean that wonderful thing you told me just before I went in to see Curtis. You must have known my knees were shaking. 'Mr. Haynes,' you said, 'I want you to know I have a book in my library that's dog-eared and loved. It's called *A Summer Ago.*' "

Ann laughed softly.

"You would remember that!"

"A book that sold exactly 622 copies," Tod added. "The one good thing I did before I became a one-shot genius. Ann—" Now his voice became quietly tense. "—hang on tight. I'm going to deliver for Curtis. I'm going up there again."

The silence came again. Now Emily could smell the magnolias; she began to feel guilty. She started to draw away from the door, filing away in her mind all she knew about the new tenants in 5B; and then Ann spoke once more.

"Tod, you didn't marry me for that, did you?"

"What?"

"Because I won't be used. I love you too much to be just the woman you need until you're on top again."

"Don't be silly."

Inside the doorway of 4B, Emily heard and nodded knowingly. Her instincts were always right. Tod Haynes wasn't the husband type.

The proof of Emily's forebodings came in due time. Each morning Ann Haynes went off to the office while her husband stayed at home, a situation Emily found deplorable.

"If he's got his wife trained to work for him, don't knock it," Sam said. But Sam didn't understand. It was dangerous to leave a man like Tod Haynes alone. He was too attractive, as was duly noted by every female in Roxbury Haven. There was Mrs. Abrams, in her late sixties, whose sole interest in Tod Haynes was because he reminded her of grandson Robert, stationed in Germany.

"With NATO," she told Tod, "very close to General Norstadt."

And Tod was so charming, Mrs. Abrams dropped a stitch on the sweater she was knitting for Robert, and Mr. Abrams raised his eyes from the *Wall Street Journal* for all of thirty seconds—more than anyone had seen of him in months.

There was Miss Fanny Brady, who had been a fixture in bit parts since the days of the crank and megaphone and would never retire. Fanny had a weakness for flame-colored capris and pink bra tops, and her hair coloring varied from orange to silver. She had no more than heard Tod's typewriter at work than she attempted to interest him in doing the story of her life.

"It won't be dull," she promised. "I have memories."

"Only memories?" Tod teased. "I should think your future would be even more interesting."

Thereafter, Miss Fanny Brady glowed every time Tod walked across the patio, or appeared on his balcony for a cigarette and coffee break.

Emily missed none of these things. Long before apartment 4B was rented, she had learned to resent Tod Haynes. She never allowed herself the luxury—or the pain—of understanding why. She never considered, as she shared a dull breakfast with Sam, that it might really be Ann Haynes whom she resented. But one thing Emily knew, by means of that ancient art known as feminine intuition, and that was that trouble came to Roxbury Haven on the day Patti Parr rented 4B.

Usually, Emily showed the apartments. Sam confined his activities to the maintenance work in morning hours before going off to his part-time job. But on the morning Patti Parr's heels clicked smartly across the patio, and her determined finger rang the bell marked "Manager," Sam adjusted his suspenders, donned the handsome Italian sweater (similar to one of Tod Haynes') Emily had given him, over protests that he wouldn't be found dead in it, and escorted Miss Parr upstairs. They were gone an inordinately long time. When Emily went up, ostensibly to see if the drapery rods were in working order, she found a merry threesome in the hall. Tod Haynes' door was open. He stood just outside chatting with Patti Parr as if they were old friends.

"I think the apartment is darling," she cried, as Emily approached, "but I wanted to see how it looked furnished. Mr. Haynes was on his balcony and heard me."

"Anything to be neighborly," Tod said. "What about it, Mrs. Proctor? Do I get a commission for renting the apartment?" And then he laughed. "Just joking. I get a new neighbor—that's commission enough."

When Patti Parr moved in, Tod Haynes was very helpful with the drapes. Emily doubted that Patti was the literary type, but he was also very helpful with the crates of books.

On one occasion, when a special-delivery package came for Patti, Emily took it up to 4B and found Tod in a strange situation. He was sprawled on the divan, a drink in one hand and a sheaf of typewritten paper in the other. He looked up when he saw her at the door. Her disapproval must have showed. He frowned—then smiled crookedly.

"Patti," he said, "shall I read that chapter to Mrs. Proctor, the one that bugged me? I told you I wanted a woman's reaction."

Patti shook her head quickly. Emily wasn't supposed to see, but she did. It was some kind of signal between them. Emily didn't understand; but she wasn't surprised when— a few days later—she heard Tod and Ann quarreling bitterly in the garage.

"Tod, I warned you," Ann said. "I won't be used!"

And Tod's voice answered, "You're making a fuss over nothing. I just had a few drinks—"

"You know what drinking did to you once—"

Discretion forbade Emily's hearing any more, but she was prepared for the big break when it came. It began with Tod's selling his book. He came home driving a black convertible; secondhand, but big. It roared magnificently down the driveway and into the garage. Moments later, Tod came striding across the patio. It was November. The rains would start any time now. Overhead, the sky was leaden. Emily began to gather up her gardening tools.

"Here, let me help you," Tod said, taking up the bag of fertilizer. "Tell me, Mrs. Proctor, do you put little umbrellas over your plants when it rains, or do you leave them standing out in the cruel world?"

Emily was a bit startled, and then she realized that Tod had been drinking again. At her door, he added, "Now, don't worry about me. I'm going right upstairs like a good boy and call my wife; and then I'm going to take her to dinner, and dancing, and we may even take a rocket to the moon."

He bounded up the stairs, leaving Emily a little breathless.

But Tod Haynes didn't go out with his wife that night. He didn't go out at all for some time.

It was almost dusk when Patti Parr came downstairs and got her small foreign car out of the garage. Midway out of the driveway, the motor stalled. Emily heard Patti trying to start it again until, finally, Tod came down and tried to help. It was no use. By that time, the rain had started. Amid much laughing, Tod pushed the small car into the garage and returned in his own. Emily saw Patti get in Tod's car and the two of them drive away.

At the usual time, Ann Haynes came home from work. Being a sensible woman, who read weather forecasts before going to work, she was wearing her hooded raincoat. Emily watched her go upstairs. After that, Emily continued to watch the Haynes' window. She saw Ann come to the balcony several times. It rained harder. As the hours passed, Emily was tortured with indecision. Should she tell poor Mrs. Haynes her husband had gone out in his car after drinking? On a rainy night, there was even more chance he might crack up. With Sam off at work, there was no one to advise her. While Emily sat beside the telephone deliberating, it rang. She picked it up.

"Mrs. Proctor," Ann Haynes asked, somewhat timidly, "I wonder if you saw my husband go out any time this afternoon?"

"Why, yes," Emily answered. "You mustn't worry, dear. He went out in his car."

"His car?" Ann Haynes echoed.

"The car he drove home. He seemed quite happy over it. And then, a little later, that sweet Miss Parr next door to you started to go out in her car, but it stalled. Your husband came down and took her—"

"Thank you!" Ann Haynes said, abruptly.

The sound of her receiver clicked in Emily's ear. She was uneasily aware, as she replaced the telephone on the cradle, that she might have said too much. But she was also aware of a vague sense of vicarious pleasure.

On the following morning, Mrs. Haynes didn't go to

work. In the middle of the morning, clear after the rain, so that all the patio regulars were in their places, Patti Parr returned in a cab. Two hours later, Tod Haynes' black convertible roared up the drive. Ten minutes later, the battle began. No one on the patio was spared any of the details, until Tod remembered the glass doors to the balcony and slammed them shut.

Emily was replacing a bulb in the lower hall when Ann Haynes came out of 5B, suitcase in hand, and started down the stairs. Tod was at her heels.

"This is insane!" he roared. "I went out to celebrate the book's being accepted. I meant to pick you up at the office, but I met an old pal—"

"Not such an old pal, according to what I heard!" Ann called over her shoulder.

"What you heard? What did you hear? It's a lie!"

"I have a witness. You'll find out in court!"

Tod came bounding down the stairs.

"I won't let you go, Ann," he insisted. "I won't let you leave me!"

But Ann left, figuratively slamming the door in Tod's face. He cursed under his breath, turned and saw Emily on the ladder. He looked at her strangely for several seconds, and then stalked back upstairs.

The look Tod had given Emily the day Ann left him was a smile compared to the sullen glare she absorbed and held with her, along with the tenant's morning mail. No one had ever given her such a fright; no one, certainly, had ever tried to run her down in the driveway. She wanted to discuss it with someone; but Sam was still asleep, and when the patio regulars appeared, Mr. Abrams buried himself behind his newspaper, and Mrs. Abrams found delight in a new letter from Robert. Fanny Brady had a new magazine, and the normalcy that came to Roxbury Haven deceived Emily into believing the two incidents were of no importance. She returned to work on the roses, only to become uneasily aware that somebody was staring at the nape of her neck. She turned, slowly. Tod Haynes was out on the balcony of 5B. He didn't have a cup of coffee; he wasn't smoking a cigarette. He was staring at her in that same malevolent manner. And even when she faced him boldly, he continued to stare. Had she been inclined to believe such things, Emily would have thought he had the Evil Eye.

After awhile, Tod went inside. Emily was relieved until that strange feeling came again, the uneasy feeling of being watched. She glanced up at the balcony. No one was there.

"Emily—"

She whirled about. Tod Haynes was standing not two feet away. It was all Emily could do to refrain from screaming.

"Oh, did I frighten you, dear?" he said warmly. "I'm sorry."

Emily was temporarily paralyzed. In spite of his familiarity with other women, Tod had never addressed her by her first name. As if that wasn't enough, he took her arm and drew her toward him.

"I just came down," he said, "to see if you would ask Sam to help me get my trunk from the garage."

"Your trunk?" Emily echoed, weakly. "Are you going away?"

Then Tod Haynes smiled in a strange and frightening way.

"We never know, do we, Emily?" he said.

Sam picked up the lunch pail and started for the door. Emily thought he was going to leave without saying anything at all. At the doorway, he looked back.

"Haynes actually tried to run you down?" he asked.

"This morning in the driveway. And I'm not making it up. The postman saw it, too. And, Sam, if you had seen the way he looked at me at the mailboxes—"

"Have you been reading other people's postcards again?"

"I wasn't *reading* anything! And then a little while ago— out on the patio." Emily lowered her voice. "He was so *familiar*."

"With you?" Sam asked.

Emily didn't like the sound of his voice. He wasn't impressed. Maybe she did look at the mail sometimes, but it was only to see where the postmarks were from. Some people had interesting friends in interesting places, not just a husband who didn't care if she was threatened and insulted.

"The way he *looks* at me," she said. "Sam, I think the divorce has affected his mind."

"He seemed all right when I took his trunk up," Sam said. "I don't know why a divorce should bother a man."

"Sam Proctor!"

But Sam was completely unsympathetic. As he turned and left her, he said, "And I've got a piece of advice for you, Emily. Don't stand around in driveways."

Sam went to work and wouldn't be back until after midnight; Emily was left with her doubts, which she tried to reason away. Mrs. Haynes had left in a rush, carrying only a bag. It wasn't unreasonable to think she'd left things behind to be packed. She listened to the sound of the trunk being dragged across the floor upstairs, and it seemed that noises were much sharper now.

A little later, another strange thing happened. Emily heard Tod Haynes come down the stairs. He went out on the patio and began to talk to old Mr. Abrams, who had been sitting in the sun alone. Nobody ever talked to Mr. Abrams. Emily's curiosity compelled her to go outside.

" . . . thirty-seven years," the old man was saying, excitedly. "Thirty-seven years in the hardware business. Tools, plumbing fixtures. Yes, sir. Anything you want to know about in the hardware line, I can tell you."

"Where can I buy a good saw?" Tod asked.

"All kinds of saws," Mr. Abrams said. "What kind of saw do you want?"

Tod hesitated. He turned slowly and saw Emily standing a few yards away. He looked at her steadily, until she began to have the same sensation she had experienced when he looked down at her from the balcony.

"What do you want the saw for?" Mr. Abrams prodded.

"When something is too large," Tod said, still staring at Emily, "it has to be cut down."

Then he walked away without saying anything more to anyone. When he came back, he carried a new saw and a coil of rope. Emily didn't see him again until after dark. In the meantine, she listened. She listened for the sound of the saw and heard nothing. She listened for the sound of the trunk and heard nothing. What she did hear was the sound of pacing. Heavy, thoughtful pacing. When she was very quiet, all the sounds in the building were magnified. She heard Patti Parr come downstairs and go off on a date. The Smiths came home. Harry Stokes came home and went out again. Still, overhead, the pacing. Once it stopped and she heard the shower run for just a few seconds. Later, there was the sound of a glass breaking in the kitchen. A few minutes later, she heard heavy footsteps come down the stairs and stop at her door. Emily didn't know she was so tense until the bell rang.

She opened the door and faced Tod Haynes.

"Emily," he said. And then he smiled, strangely. "I knew you would be waiting by the door."

He had been drinking. His hair was mussed and his tie awry. When he took a step forward, she leaned on the door.

"Don't be afraid of me, Emily," he said. "I'm not going to come in." He carried a bundle which he shifted from one arm to another. "Laundry," he explained. "Keep forgetting to take it out now that I'm a bachelor again . . . Emily, I know how you notice things, so I thought I'd save you some trouble. There's a woman coming to my apartment tonight. No, don't say anything yet," he protested, as her mouth opened. "I'm telling you because she may come while I'm out, and I don't want you worrying your mind about it. You worry about all of us so much."

When Emily found her voice, it was unexpectedly shrill.

"Mr. Haynes," she said, "you've been drinking."

"I know," Tod answered. "It's terrible, isn't it? I have all kinds of bad habits—like giving a pretty girl a ride when her car won't start."

"And not coming back until the next day!"

Tod beamed. "There, I knew you hadn't missed that! Who else could have known, I asked myself. Who else but dear Emily?"

There was nothing happy in his smile. Behind it, in his eyes, was that same look that had frightened her all day.

"Mr. Haynes," she said firmly, "you can't blame me for your misconduct."

"Indeed I can't," he confessed. "Indeed I can't. But when the woman I'm expecting comes—if she comes before I get back—just close your eyes and let her go upstairs unmolested—please. She'll have a key. She's only coming to pick up her trunk."

"Do you mean it's your wife?" Emily asked.

Tod shook his head sadly.

"Emily, dear," he said. "I have no wife. . . . "

His words trailed behind him as he walked away. Not until he was gone did Emily begin to wonder how Ann Haynes was going to carry that large trunk downstairs.

It was almost two hours later that Emily heard the sound of footsteps on the patio. She scurried to the window and peeked out to see Mrs. Haynes, wearing her familiar hooded raincoat, enter the building. The footsteps went up the stairs. Moments later, the door opened and Mrs. Haynes walked inside. She proceeded slowly through the apartment. Emily waited for the sound of the trunk that didn't come. After a few moments, the footsteps went out on the balcony. Quietly, Emily slid open her door. Now she caught the smell of a cigarette. Then the sound came—a quick gasp of surprise.

"I thought you were smarter than that," Tod said quietly. "Did you think I was going to let you get away with it?"

There was no time for an answer. While Emily stood frozen below, thinking Tod must have returned without her knowing it, there was a dull thud, a scraping sound and the quick closing of the glass doors. Simultaneously, a tiny red spark spiraled down from above and dropped at her feet.

She picked it up. It was a cigarette, still smoldering and marked with lip rouge.

Emily hurried inside and locked the door behind her. She hardly dared to breathe. Her mind raced back over the day: the anger in Tod's face when he came home from court; the incident in the driveway; his strange changes of mood; the trunk, the rope and the saw—At that point her mind balked. Then she heard the sounds again: a scuffling, something that might have been a chair being moved, a crash—finally, a heavy thud that made the ceiling shudder.

She waited. It was all over. No. Now the pacing began again. When it stopped, she heard the trunk being dragged across the floor; after that, more pacing. Then the shower began to run—hard. It ran for a long time. What was the shower for? To wash away—what? Alone in her world of sounds, Emily panicked. She ran to the telephone. The police? She hesitated. That might be brash. Sam. Yes, she'd call Sam at work and try to make him understand. And then she stopped, telephone in hand. The shower was still running, but now there was a closer sound. The door directly above slammed shut, and heavy footsteps came down the stairs. They stopped in front of her door, and there was a silence of several seconds before they slowly walked away. Emily dropped the telephone into the cradle and hurried to the window. Tod Haynes was crossing the patio. His shoulders sagged and his head was down, and under one arm he carried something wrapped in a newspaper. It could have been a saw.

Emily was terrified, but she had to know. She waited until he disappeared down the driveway; then she got the pass key. She slipped upstairs unnoticed and unlocked the door of 5B. Inside, all was darkness except for the light showing in the bathroom. She waited until her eyes adjusted to the shadows. Standing near the door was a trunk. Around it, tied tightly, was the rope. Hanging from the rope was a shipping tag addressed—as she could see by the light from the bathroom—to Mrs. Haynes. She moved forward, giving the trunk a wide margin. The bathroom was a magnet. Proceeding toward it, her foot touched something glittering on the floor. She picked it up. It was a liquor glass, still smelling of whisky.

Emily stepped inside the bathroom. The shower was going at full pressure; steam billowed over the top of the enclosure until it was difficult to see across the small room. She had to learn what was behind those frosted doors; but, for the moment, she was paralyzed. Nowhere in her journey to the shower had she seen anything of Mrs. Haynes.

But Emily wasn't alone in the apartment. She knew that the instant the bathroom door slammed shut behind her. She screamed and whirled about. The doorknob was still turning. She grabbed it with both hands and pulled with all her strength against whoever might be outside—trying to pull it open—until her fingers found the lock . . .

Emily's scream was penetrating, and it went on for a long time. Long enough for all the residents of Roxbury Haven to crowd outside apartment 5B, where they stood helpless before a locked door until Tod Haynes came bounding up the stairs two steps at a time. As he hurriedly unlocked the door, the two policemen Fanny Brady had thoughtfully summoned from a passing patrol car, shouldered through the group. They went directly to the bathroom, the source of the now weakening screams, and pounded on the door with an authority that brought response. Bedraggled, dripping and babbling hysterically, Emily emerged from the steaming interior.

"Why, Mrs. Proctor," Tod exclaimed, "whatever have you been doing in my shower?"

She stared at him—horrified.

"Murderer!" she gasped.

All around Emily was a tight ring of faces—her incredulous and astonished tenants. Nobody seemed to understand.

"Murderer!" she repeated. "He cut her up in the shower with a saw. He's got her remains stuffed in a trunk!"

Tod Haynes said nothing at all. One of the policemen went into the bathroom and turned off the shower, revealing a stall completely free of bloodstains or bone fragments. The saw was found on the kitchen sink.

"I got it to trim that magnolia branch hanging over the balcony," Tod explained. "It's been knocking me in the head for a year."

Now everything seemed to be happening in a dream. One of the officers peeked outside and came back rubbing his forehead where it had contacted the magnolia tree. That left only the trunk—which was opened to reveal nothing but Mrs. Haynes clothing, including the hooded raincoat. While truth seeped slowly through the confusion in Emily's mind, Tod casually lit a cigarette, glanced at the mouthpiece and then wiped the last trace of lipstick from a corner of his mouth.

"It was you!" Emily cried. "You're the one who came back! You're Mrs. Haynes!"

Everybody stared at Emily, strangely.

"I think we've got a live one," said the officer who took Emily's arm. "Come along, lady. I know a nice doctor who'll enjoy talking to you."

Emily was helpless. She felt herself being drawn along through the group of her astonished tenants, and she knew Tod Haynes had contrived the whole affair in order to discredit her. Nobody, she was sure, would ever believe anything she said again.

But at the doorway, they were stopped by a man in a raincoat who was almost as confused as Emily.

"I've been ringing the bell downstairs," he said, "but nobody answers. I've got a subpoena for—" He paused to read from the paper in his hand. "—Mrs. Emily Proctor— witness: Haynes *versus* Haynes."

Emily looked quickly at Tod—in time to catch what no one else saw or could have understood: a smile of deep satisfaction.

I'M BETTER THAN YOU   Henry Slesar

NICKI WASN'T HOME when the telephone call came and the roommate who took the message was too flustered to make a coherent report. She wasn't sure about *where* Mr. Wolfe had seen Nicki perform: summer stock or the two-minute walk-on in *Gypsy* or the television commercial for that upholstery cleanser; but what was the difference? Nicki was supposed to go to the Broadhurst Theatre at four *prompt*, if she wanted a reading. Nicki was so flustered that she burst out of the rooming house without even passing a comb through her tangled blonde hair. She walked the thirteen blocks to the theatre, not allowing herself the indulgence of a taxi ride. It might be a job, sure, but the casting had been in progress for over a month, and nothing could be left but the smallest of parts.

There were only five people on stage when Nicki walked in, and four of them barely glanced up when she stepped hesitantly onto the boards. The fifth, a youngish, bony-headed man in a pullover, grinned and came over. She knew it was Wolfe, the director, an import from a downtown theatre who was making his Broadway start with a new comedy.

"I know you," he said. "You're Nicki Porter. Thanks for coming."

"Thank *you*, Mr. Wolfe," she said shyly, using her full-throated voice well. Nicki wasn't outstandingly pretty or even provocatively plain; her best feature was her voice.

"I'll tell you what this is," Wolfe said. "There's a young widow in this play, very young, not exactly the mourner type. The part's pretty small, but it's the kind of thing that gets noticed. Hey, Jerry," he called to the heavy-set man talking earnestly to a handsome woman in blue slacks. "Toss me a script."

Nicki fingered the pages eagerly, and the director said, "Try the speech on page twelve, Mary Lou's speech. She's a Southern type, but we don't want any fried-chicken accent." He started to walk off, but stopped to say, "Oh, look, Nicki, I want to make something clear. Frankly, we stopped casting the show last Friday. The only part I was dubious about was Mary Lou's, and we sort of settled on somebody. Then I remembered seeing you in something or other at Watkins Glen—"

"Voice of the Turtle."

"That's right. Anyway, you kind of *looked* like Mary Lou in that, so I traced you through Equity. But don't get *too* hopeful about this, because who knows?" He shrugged, sharing with her his understanding of the theatre's uncertainty.

The speech on page twelve was meaty. She knew she was reading well, and when she was through, the woman in the blue slacks struck her hands together in light, approving applause.

"Well, fine," Wolfe said with a sigh. "That's just fine, Nicki. We won't keep you waiting for the decision very long; rehearsals have to start next week." He flashed a smile. "Where's my manners? Want you to meet the gang." He propelled her towards the group, and tossed off the prominent theatrical names as if they were casual guests in somebody's living room. Nicki shook hands, fighting the flush that was rising and spreading to the tips of her exposed ears. She was always this way, shy and tongue-tied before the easy-mannered people who knew the rewards of theatrical success. They were the anchored ones, solidly fixed on what seemed to her to be a capricious and treacherous ocean. As she left the theatre, she felt like a small craft drifting out to sea.

But the watery analogies that filled her mind vanished once the stage door closed behind her. The solid reality of the sidewalk brought her with a bump to the realization that she had been liked, really liked, and that the part was going to be hers. She turned and looked again at the theatre posters, and when she saw the young, dark-haired girl coming out of the lobby pause to look at her, she felt an impulse to run up to this stranger and babble out the story of her sudden hopefulness. Instead, she turned and headed for the cafeteria on the corner.

She was about ready for her second cup of coffee when she spotted the dark-haired girl just three tables away, looking as if she expected an invitation. Nicki smiled, just a small smile that could be construed as a private pleasantry or an acknowledgment. The girl must have taken it the latter way; she picked up her purse and came over.

"May I sit down?" she said. There was a breathless quality in her voice, and her white teeth were biting her lower lip. She was pretty, Nicki thought, in a pinched-face Julie Harris way, but her eyes were swollen, even protruding. "I'd like to talk to you a minute," she said.

"Sure," Nicki said, moving things closer to her side of the small table. "I think I saw you at the theatre—"

"Yes," she said, sitting down. "I was there, but please don't mention it, not to Mr. Wolfe, I mean. You see, I'm Jill Yarborough, maybe Mr. Wolfe mentioned me."

"No, he didn't."

"Not even that?" She made herself laugh, and it struck Nicki as being theatrical.

"Are you an actress?"

"That's what I keep telling them. I was sitting in back of the theatre during your reading. You were pretty good, I thought. I couldn't hear you too well, you weren't projecting, but I think you were good."

"Thanks," Nicki said, stirring uncomfortably and suddenly afraid of the heat content in the girl's eyes.

"I'm surprised Mr. Wolfe didn't say anything about me, because he practically promised me the part last Friday. The Mary Lou part. You wouldn't know it to listen to me, but I'm from the South, deep South, that is, but I've been North so long you can hardly tell by my accent. Can you?"

"No."

"Well, I worked like crazy to get rid of my drawl, and then *this* thing comes along. Wouldn't it kill you?" She put a gloved hand to her lips as if to stifle a giggle, but there wasn't any. "I haven't had a *real* job, an acting job I mean, for almost a year. When Wolfe said I was just what he was looking for, I could have crowed like a rooster. Only then he called me Saturday morning and said he wasn't sure yet. That was a lousy Saturday morning, let me tell you."

"I'm sorry, Miss—"

"Yarborough. Only call me Jill. Your name's Nicki?"

"Yes."

"Well, I didn't turn on the oven or anything," Jill Yarborough said, her eyes staring through Nicki's forehead. "But I didn't crow anymore either. I thought I'd hang around the theatre today, just to see what would happen. And I saw."

Nicki wanted to touch the girl's hand, or do something to mitigate the pain in her voice. But all she could do was answer in choked tones.

"I'm sorry," she said. "I know how it is, too. I've been sitting in casting offices for the last eight months myself. But I don't think anything's definite about this—"

Jill Yarborough laughed. "Oh, come on. You ought to be able to tell. He *likes* you, Nicki. That's for sure." The smile went. "Only I'm better than you are. Better for the part, better in every way."

Nicki, embarrassed, looked into her empty cup. The girl didn't say anything else for awhile, but her swollen eyes were still on Nicki's face, and she could hear her breath clearly, even in the clatter of the restaurant. Then she said, her voice so low that Nicki had to strain to hear:

"Don't take the job. Nicki. Tell him you can't take it."

"What?"

"Don't take the part. Call up Mr. Wolfe and tell him you don't want it. That there's something else you have to do, that you've got a conflict."

It was a shock to hear the blatant words, the unashamed suggestion.

"You can't be serious?"

"I am. I *am*. I'm better than you are, Nicki, I've worked harder. You don't deserve it the way I do."

"But *I* need the work, too. You can't—"

"Not like I need it. Not the way I do. You couldn't." The girl shut her eyes, and the action was merciful, like a shade pulled down over a glaring window light. Then her eyes opened and she said, "If you take the part, I'll kill you. So help me, Nicki, that's what I'll do."

Nicki gasped, and scraped back her chair.

"I'll kill you and then I'll kill myself. I've thought of doing that for a long time anyway. I gave myself this one last chance, and that's all. I was going to take this."

She fumbled in her purse. Half-hidden in her trembling fingers she exposed a small, dark-brown bottle, the skull and crossbones clearly outlined at the bottom of the label.

"You can't threaten me," Nicki said in a whisper. "I won't let you scare me out of taking the—"

"I'm not trying to scare you. I'm just telling you the fact. You say yes to Wolfe, and we both die. If you want to tell the police about this, you go ahead and see what it gets you. I'll laugh my head off and say that you're crazy, see what good it does you."

She rose swiftly from the table, turning her head as if to avoid a display of tears, and gathered up her purse and the single glove she had yanked off her hand in her nervousness. Then she dropped half a dollar on the table and went hurriedly to the revolving doors.

It wasn't a matter of calculating her decision. It was being made for Nicki in some busy chamber of her mind, all the time she walked back to the rooming house, and all through the excited conversation with Theresa, the friend who shared her room and her aspirations. She didn't even mention Jill Yarborough; she wasn't going to be bluffed out of her first real break in almost a year.

At eight-thirty the next morning, the telephone rang. Nicki pushed pillows off her bed and fumbled for the receiver.

"Nicki? This is Carl Wolfe—"

She shut her eyes and prayed.

"If you like us, we like you," the director said. "We're having the first meeting of the cast Tuesday morning at ten. Can you be there?"

"Oh, sure," Nicki said casually. Then she hung up, walked nonchalantly around the bed, picked up the pillow, and thumped the back of her sleeping roommate. "Wake up, you fool!" she screamed ecstatically. "I got the job!"

She forgot about Jill Yarborough. Memorizing her three-page part made her forget. Carl Wolfe, gracious, demanding, and biting at the first meeting she attended, made her forget. And then, a faltering first-time "blocking" rehearsal, followed by a triumphant run-through that Wolfe grudgingly called "pretty near perfect," made her forget the burning, protruding eyes, the small brown bottle, the agony and threat of Jill Yarborough.

On Wednesday night, she walked home from the theatre at seven-thirty, tired but still elated. Theresa had wanted them to go out that evening; she had a boyfriend named Freddy, and Freddy had a friend who'd *love* to meet an honest-to-God working actress, but Nicki had refused. When she used the key to the apartment, she walked into darkness and solitude. She undressed, washed her hair, put on a housecoat, and flopped on the sofa with a book. When the doorbell rang, she got up to answer it without hesitation, because Nicki had forgotten about Jill Yarborough.

She was wearing a long black coat with a fake fur collar high around the neck, clasped by a nervously working hand. She said Nicki's name, and Nicki almost moved to slam the door on her, but she didn't. The girl walked in.

"Wasn't easy finding you," she said. "I had to ask the stage doorman—"

"Please don't make any trouble," Nicki said wearily. "It's all settled now. There's no need to make a scene, Miss Yarborough—"

"Call me Jill," the girl said. She looked around the apartment briefly, and then moved to take off her coat. For a moment, Nicki thought it was going to be all right. Her manner was relaxed, casual. She dropped the coat on a chair. "It's a nice place," she said. "Do you live here alone?"

"I have a roommate. She should be back any minute. . . ."

Jill Yarborough smiled. "I'll bet she won't. I'll bet she's got a date, and you haven't. I know how it is when you're working. You don't even care if there's a man in your life. Isn't that true?"

"I— was too tired to go out tonight."

"Naturally." The girl sat, folding her hands primly in her lap; until then, Nicki had been afraid to meet her eyes. Now she did, and saw that their hot light was undiminished since the time of their first meeting. "How did the first rehearsal go?" she said lightly.

"All right, I suppose."

"He's a funny guy, isn't he? That Carl Wolfe, I mean. One minute he's sweet as pie; the next, he's chewing you out like a top sergeant. I've heard about him."

"He's really very nice."

The girl smiled again, sleepily. "I'll bet you thought I didn't mean what I said to you that time. Did you?"

"You were upset that day—"

Jill Yarborough shifted the coat onto her lap. Her hand dipped into a pocket. Nicki, on the sofa, stiffened. The hand came out with the brown bottle.

"Oh, I meant it," the girl said dreamily. "I meant every word. I was going to kill you, and then myself."

"Please," Nicki said anxiously. "Don't do anything foolish that—"

"You thought I was only bluffing, but I wasn't. I was right for that part. I'm a better actress than you are, a whole lot better. You know what's wrong with you?" she asked, matter-of-factly. "You're all voice and no body. You only act with your larynx." She turned the bottle around in her hand. "I'm going to make you drink this," she said.

Nicki squirmed to the edge of the sofa and stood up. "I'll scream," she whispered. "If you try anything I'll scream the house down. There are people right next door . . . "

"You don't have what it takes," Jill Yarborough said bitterly. "You're not willing to fight for a part, not the way I am. To get someplace in the theatre, you have to be a little mad, and you have to be able to fight every step of the way. That's why I'm better than you, Nicki."

She uncorked the bottle.

"Get out of here!" Nicki yelled.

Jill Yarborough grinned, and stood up. She came forward, her shoulders hunched, her eyes and teeth grotesquely white in her dark, tormented face. She moved slowly, a dream figure, nightmarish.

"This is for you, Nicki," she said, holding up the bottle. "For you . . . "

Nicki screamed.

The girl stopped, and her face changed. She put her shaking hand to her forehead; the heat in her eyes faded. Then she caught her breath, and tipped the mouth of the small bottle to her lips. She threw back her head, and the contents disappeared down her throat. She swallowed hard, painfully, and let the bottle drop from her fingers and bounce on the carpet. Nicki screamed again and covered her eyes; when she looked once more, Jill Yarborough hadn't moved, stunned by her own action. Nicki, sobbing, went to her.

"Get away from me," the girl said hoarsely. "You got what you wanted, get away." She took a step, and her knees buckled. "Oh, God, it hurts," she said, holding her stomach.

"I'll get a doctor—"

"Stay where you are!"

"You've got to let me help you!"

Jill Yarborough went to the sofa, leaning against its arm. She began to retch, and sank to her knees. It was then that Nicki grabbed the telephone.

The interns who took Jill Yarborough into Nicki's bedroom were both young, cool, and taciturn. There were strangled sounds behind the closed bedroom door for almost an hour; Nicki sat quaking on the sofa in the living room, waiting for word.

Finally, one of the interns emerged, a crisp young man with blond hair. The ordeal over, he was more willing to be friendly. When Nicki babbled her questions at him, he grinned.

"She'll be okay," he said. "Good as new in a day or two. We used the stomach pump and gave her a sedative." He sat down and lit a cigarette. "There's something I have to ask you now. Something rather important."

"Yes?"

"The girl claims she thought she was drinking cough syrup, that the whole business was a mistake. Were you here at the time it happened?"

"Yes, I was."

He considered her thoughtfully. "You know if she swallowed that stuff deliberately, we'd have to report it to the police. Suicide's a crime in this state."

"You mean, she'd be arrested?"

"Not as bad as all that. She'd be sent to an observation ward in one of the city hospitals, so we'd keep an eye on her, give a psychiatric checkup. These suicide types, they don't quit on the first try." He eyed her speculatively. "Could you corroborate her story, Miss?"

"Yes," Nicki said, looking away. "It was purely an accident. She had no reason to commit suicide, none at all."

When the ambulance had gone, Nicki tried calling the Broadhurst, but there was no answer. She found Carl Wolfe's telephone number in the directory and, luckily, he was home. He listened to her opening statements in silence.

"It's just something I can't help," she said. "I'll have to be out of town for the next few weeks, and that means I won't be available for rehearsals. So maybe it's best we call it off."

"I understand," Wolfe said, finally. "I'm sorry about this, Nicki. I think you were right for the part. Maybe some other time . . . "

"You have someone else in mind, don't you? I wouldn't want you to be stranded or anything like that."

"Yes," Wolfe said, "we do have another candidate. The one I was giving the part to until you came along."

Thank God, Nicki thought. Then she said a quick goodbye and hung up.

She tiptoed quietly into the bedroom. The girl was still asleep, but she stirred and opened her eyes as Nicki approached the bed.

"I've called Carl Wolfe," Nicki said coldly. "Can you hear me, Jill? I called Carl Wolfe and said I didn't want the part. It's all yours," she said bitterly. "I don't want it half as much as you do."

Jill Yarborough smiled. "I'm better than you are," she said softly. "I deserve the part. Didn't I prove it to you? Didn't I?"

"What do you mean?"

"I nearly died," Jill Yarborough said, and then laughed raspingly. "Could you swallow water and nearly die? That's all it was, you know. Water! Could you do it? Could you?" She struggled to sit up, and Nicki backed away from the bed. "Could you?" Jill Yarborough screamed at her, in rage, in righteousness, and in exultant triumph.

A SIMPLE UNCOMPLICATED MURDER C. B. Gilford

THE MURDER which Norman Landers committed was ideal in so many respects. A classic murder, you might say, one for a textbook on the subject.

The victim, first of all, was a relative, which fact allowed Norman complete knowledge of his habits, weaknesses, etc. The motive was twofold—money and a woman—and therefore unimpeachable. The performance of the crime was ridiculously safe and easy—and therefore involved scarcely any problems of alibi, escape, and that sort of thing. All in all, it was such a golden opportunity that Norman Landers, not a born murderer by any means, not really constitutionally suited for violence and bloody deeds, simply could not resist the temptation.

Was it a perfect crime, however? Despite all the fortuitous circumstances, did Norman Landers escape detection and punishment, and did he really reap the rewards of his bold adventure?

There's the real question. And not an easy question to answer. At least the answer is somewhat equivocal, rather than a simple and easy yes or no.

First of all, there were the two cousins, Norman and Arnold. Both were surnamed Landers. There'd been a high rate of mortality in the family, and both were reared by their Aunt Elizabeth. Reared from something of a distance, that is. They spent their youths in boarding schools, sometimes different, sometimes the same one. Then finally they both attended and graduated from a swanky Eastern university. Shortly afterwards, Aunt Elizabeth conveniently died. A natural death, incidentally. There is no reason to believe otherwise.

That was in 1928. Aunt Elizabeth left each young man about a hundred and fifty thousand apiece. That's big money, and it was even bigger in those days.

The next year, as fate would have it, was 1929. Norman had imagined himself something of a financier. The crash proved otherwise. A year after becoming rich, he was dead broke.

Arnold was more fortunate. He'd kept his money in cold cash, and so the depression made him a richer man by comparison than he'd been before. He was rich and he was a solid citizen, and as such it was rather natural for him to marry.

That brought Clare Kimberly into the picture. Clare was a charmer. A natural blonde with a stunning figure, she was college-bred and cultured, yet with just enough of the wild flapper in her to make that particular combination of lady and trollop which is irresistible to almost any man. And she was beautiful besides.

Arnold Landers found her and fell in love with her. But Norman, who lived now off Arnold's charity and so was never too far distant from his cousin, saw her and fell in love with her too. He even courted her in an oblique sort of way. Of course, being a pauper, he had no real chance. Clare Kimberly, whomever she might have preferred at the time, chose to marry Arnold.

The wedding was in 1931, and two years later, a boy— the only child they would ever have—was born to them. He was christened Euin.

In 1940, Arnold Landers' luck ran out and he was stricken with a disease which eventually left him partially paralyzed, confined to a wheelchair, and in more or less constant pain of varying degrees. The pain required the regular use of a palliative drug.

The stage was set for a murder.

Norman Landers came to realize the situation only gradually. He didn't jump to the immediate conclusion that murder was his best course. He wasn't that bloodthirsty. Rather the opportunity was thrust upon him, and it soon became a necessity.

He arrived to reside permanently at Arnold's home shortly after his cousin was stricken. It was Arnold's idea. There ought to be a healthy man around the house. It was safer, for one thing. Safer . . .

"You don't mind, do you, Norm?" the sick man wanted to know. "Living here, I mean."

Norman considered. His own diggings consisted of a single room in a cheap boardinghouse. He'd been drifting from boring job to boring job, and was currently unemployed. "No, I don't mind," he answered. "I have nothing better to do."

He couldn't tell at this point exactly what Clare's attitude toward him was. She'd been hard hit by Arnold's illness. She'd been a gay girl and later she'd become a gay young matron. She hadn't seemed too unhappy that there'd been only one child. Having one child was less of a burden than having many. She could still have her parties and good times. Then Arnold's illness spoiled it all. She was selfish, but she wasn't quite selfish and unfeeling enough to go on leading her old life without her husband.

"Arnold has asked me to come and live here, Clare," Norman told her. "How does that strike you?"

She gave him an odd look. Now at thirty she was more beautiful than ever. Her eyes had darkened, it seemed, but they were still blue, and there were just a few tiny lines around them. Her hair was still gloriously blonde, and her figure, if possible, had improved with ripening.

"Do you think it's wise?" she asked finally. "Considering every aspect, that is."

He knew what she meant, and he loved her for it. She

was remembering how fond he'd been of her, and she was thinking—so it seemed—of his welfare, not her own.

"Arnold wants me to come here," he said, "because the place needs a man. As a sort of caretaker. I won't be anything more than that."

You see how innocent his intentions were at this point. He wasn't presuming to become Clare's lover, and he certainly wasn't planning murder.

When he checked with the last person involved, little Euin, the results were somewhat different, more difficult, more puzzling. He found the boy out on the wide lawn playing with his black Scotty.

On Norman's deliberately hearty greeting, the boy scarcely glanced up, but went on tickling the dog's ears. He was a handsome lad with his mother's blonde coloring. He had inherited both her beauty and gaiety rather than the plodding straightforwardness and the dourer look of the Landers side.

"Euin," Norman said, "your father wants me to come and live with all of you in this house."

"Why?" the boy asked.

"To have an able-bodied man around the place. While your father is sick, that is."

"I'm an able-bodied man," the boy said.

Norman placated. "Well, you will be before long. I think your father wants me to stay for just awhile, till you get just a little bigger and can take over."

The boy's eyes, blue as his mother's, came up and stared into Norman's face. "All right," he answered, "if my father says so. But just till I'm bigger."

Norman hesitated. He had had few dealings with Euin, had never gotten close to him. Now suddenly he realized that Euin was an individual, even if he was only eight, an individual with opinions of his own. And one of those opinions was pretty clear. Euin didn't particularly like his Uncle Norman.

But Norman brazened it out with false heartiness. "That's a deal, Euin. I'll stay just till you're bigger."

When the war came, Norman managed to avoid service on the grounds of age and the fact that he had the responsibility of his cousin's family. He stayed on at Arnold's house. Despite the fact of Euin's growth, that is. And despite the continuing fact of Euin's quiet, nonviolent, unspoken hostility.

Because it had begun to be apparent to Norman that he didn't want to leave. What had been an uneasy acceptance of a difficult situation with Clare had changed gradually to a desire to improve that situation.

Clare was obviously unhappy. She was still loyal to Arnold. There was no affair between her and Norman. But there arose between them a kind of silent understanding. Or at least Norman imagined there was an understanding. If it weren't for Arnold, Clare would have him. He was sure of that. In fact, Arnold, with his incurable disease, was already out of the picture. Except, of course, that he wasn't. He was dead, but not officially.

Norman began to brood and to watch Arnold. The latter had begun to forsake the more active life of the wheelchair, and to spend more and more of his time in bed. He was sinking, Norman guessed, and the doctors confirmed that fact. But he was a long way from being dead. The doctors confirmed that fact too.

Why doesn't he die? Norman asked himself this unanswerable question a dozen times every day. I want his money, I want his house, I want his wife. And his wife wants me.

But it wasn't just a matter of greed and lust. Norman didn't use those harsh terms, of course, to describe his own motivation. It was a matter of mercy, too. Arnold was in pain. Sometimes terrible pain. So terrible on occasion that not even the drug he used completely alleviated it. Arnold ought to die for his own sake.

But he didn't die.

Norman grew more and more hard pressed to conceal his impatience and irritation. He was spending a great deal of time with Arnold now. He was the only person around

who was strong enough to lift the sick man from his bed
to his chair and back again from chair to bed. And Arnold
seemed to crave his cousin's company somehow, even more
than his wife's or his son's.

"I don't know what I'd do without you, Norm," he said
often. "Clare could never have handled this by herself, you
know. And as for Euin, I'd just as soon he wouldn't see too
much of me like this. I'd rather he wouldn't remember his
father so vividly as a cripple."

At this hint of imminent, expected death in Arnold's conversation, Norman would always perk up. "You don't sound
very hopeful," he'd chide.

"Hopeful? I'm a condemned man."

"But you don't feel any worse, do you?"

"I can scarcely feel any worse, Norm. The pain gets so
bad sometimes I wonder if I can stand it."

Then put an end to it, Norman wanted to scream.
There's that poisonous drug right on the table beside you.
Why don't you take an overdose?

"Isn't there anything to be done, Arnold?" he asked
aloud one day finally.

"What can be done? All the doctors . . . "

"I don't mean the doctors."

"Who then?"

"You yourself. The doctors said to take just so much of
that stuff. But if that amount isn't enough, why not . . . ?"

He couldn't finish. He'd been too bold and too careless
already. The suggestion needed to be more indirect, more
subtle. He'd already botched it.

"Do you actually mean suicide, Norman?"

"Well, not exactly . . . "

"What do you mean then?"

"I don't know . . . forget I said it . . . "

But obviously Arnold wasn't going to forget it. He lay
staring at his cousin, and it was there, definitely, shining
bright in his eyes—fear.

Desperately, Norman tried to change the subject. But
Arnold wouldn't permit it. And as Norman paced the

room, Arnold's eyes followed him. Finally, to escape those eyes, Norman invented an excuse and left the room.

He had to be alone to think, and to fight down his panic. He knew very well what he had done. It wasn't so much that he had suggested suicide to Arnold. But in so doing, he had revealed his own motivations. Arnold's fearful eyes had showed plainly that he understood, understood how Norman wanted to take his place, his place at the head of the manorial table, his place with Clare.

And sooner or later, Arnold would confide his fear to someone. So he had to be stopped and quickly.

That evening Norman put into Arnold's glass five times the recommended dosage of the pain-killing drug. And he stood over the bed while his cousin in a semi-stupor, partly induced by the onslaught of pain, drained off the concoction.

Then he retired to his own bed. But he didn't sleep immediately. He lay awake listening for suspicious sounds from Arnold's room, which was right next to his. He heard Clare go in to say good night to her husband. But he judged from the fact that she stayed only a moment, that neither had Arnold told her anything nor had his condition seemed alarming yet. Later, perhaps toward dawn, from sheer nervous exhaustion, Norman finally slept.

When he awoke, the sun was streaming light through his windows, and there was a small knocking at his door. He hastily put on a robe over his pajamas and went to answer the knock. He found Euin, dressed and looking grave, on his threshold.

It took Norman a full minute to recover from his surprise. The boy had never before sought out his company. His visit now could only portend disaster.

But as always in dealing with the boy, though he knew he never fooled him, Norman finally managed cheeriness. "Come in, Euin, come in."

"I don't care to come in," the boy said. "I just wanted to tell you something."

"Well all right, tell me."

"I've been talking to my father."

Battling for self-control, Norman tried to turn the conversation. "You shouldn't bother your father at this time of the morning. He needs his sleep . . . "

"I always sneak in to see him early in the morning, Uncle Norman. Then there's never anybody to chase me out. My father and I had a long talk this morning."

Norman clutched his fists till the nails dug painfully into the palms. "Well, what did you talk about?"

"My father told me he was dying."

"Dying! I must go and . . . "

Norman tried to brush past the boy, but the latter stopped him with a curt interruption. "You don't need to go and see, Uncle Norman. My father is already dead."

The police detective, a man named Giardello, was kindly and unsuspicious. He reported to the family that the death had indeed occurred from an overdose of the pain-killing drug. He apparently presumed, without its being suggested to him, that the drug had been self-administered.

But he did ask a few routine questions—of Norman, then of Clare, and finally of Euin. The detective phrased these last questions carefully, so as not to suggest to the young mind the ugly idea of suicide.

"Now what exactly did your father say to you?"

"That he was dying."

"Did you know what that word meant?"

"Yes, my father explained it to me."

"What else did he say to you about dying? Did he say, for instance, that he *wanted* to die?"

"No, sir."

"Well, did he say anything that we . . . your . . . mother ought to know?"

The boy hesitated, and Norman waited for the blow to fall. There was no doubt in his mind that Arnold, if he had indeed talked to his son just before he died, would certainly have told him that Uncle Norman wanted him dead and that Uncle Norman had given him the overdose.

"Well, what did he say?" the detective urged gently.

Euin glanced up at his questioner, and then very slowly and deliberately he turned his gaze to Norman. They stared at each other for a long moment, and to Norman, who tried desperately to read a meaning there, the boy's eyes were blank and enigmatic. He felt helpless, absolutely helpless, his entire fate in this child's hands.

In despair, he echoed the detective's question. "Tell the man what your father said. . . . "

"Oh, he told me things all right," the boy answered solemnly. "But they were things just between me and him."

It was Clare who put a stop to it. "Let him alone, please let him alone," she begged. She was pretty unnerved herself.

"Sure thing," the policeman agreed, and in ten minutes he was gone.

Norman watched his exit without being able to believe his good luck. Clare had gone out of the room, but Euin still lingered. He had taken a book down from the shelves, and was idly flipping pages. Not reading, just playing. The turning pages made a rhythmic whisper.

Norman couldn't bear the suspense any longer. "Why didn't you tell the policeman?" he demanded.

"Tell him what?"

"What you and your father talked about."

Again the blank stare. Was it mysterious, or was it really blank? Had Arnold told the boy anything or hadn't he? Would he perhaps have wanted to spare him so ugly a thing as murder in the family? Because surely Arnold himself must have realized why he was dying and at whose hand.

"My father and I," the boy said, "talked about things that were just between the two of us."

Norman hadn't stayed on at Clare's house. It was improper now, he reasoned. But of course he was always close by, and took care of household matters as he'd done before.

He had no choice about it really. He would have liked

to go away, but how could he? He had no money, no skill whatsoever at providing himself with the necessities of life. So he had to stay. And once he decided that, other decisions came automatically. If he had to stay, he might as well make the best of it. Which meant proceeding with his original plans.

When, after the proper year had passed and he proposed marriage to Clare, her eager acceptance was spoiled just a little bit by a sudden coyness. "I'll marry you, Norm," she said, "if Euin gives his permission."

"Euin?"

"Yes, you'll have to ask Euin for my hand."

If she hadn't been so exquisite, so desirable, and if he had had any other choice but to desire her, he might have refused to cooperate in such nonsense. As it was, he tried to talk her out of it.

"No, darling," she insisted, "you simply must talk to Euin first. After all, remember he had Arnold's last confidence. Maybe Arnold told him his final wish concerning my remarriage."

Norman shuddered. "That's a ghastly notion," he said.

"Not ghastly, darling. Ghostly." Then she covered his mouth with her own so he couldn't reply.

He sought out Euin that evening in the library. The boy had taken to reading a lot, and could usually be found there any evening after dinner. Norman felt stupid, coming to a thirteen-year-old boy with a question like his. And he also felt afraid. This was just the kind of occasion which might unlock the boy's silence.

"Euin," he began, "I've proposed marriage to your mother and she's accepted me. Do you have any objection?"

The boy stopped reading, but instead of looking up, commenced flipping the pages of the book. It was a maddening little habit he'd acquired, and he seemed to do it whenever Norman spoke to him and he happened to have a book.

"Why should I have any objections?" he countered.

"Well, I thought your first objection might be the fact that you didn't like me."

The boy still played with the book. "Whatever gave you that idea, Uncle Norman?"

The boy also had an unfailing capacity for making Norman feel cheap and inferior. "Look here, we might as well admit it, to each other at least. You never have liked me. . . . "

Euin closed the book with a sudden snap. "All right, Uncle, I'll admit it. I don't like you."

"Then you do object to my marrying your mother."

"No, I don't."

"Why not?"

The boy looked directly at the man now. He seemed much older than thirteen. But then he'd lived so much in a world of adults, with so few playmates his own age. Perhaps it was natural.

"I think you should marry my mother," he said, "because I think my mother wants to marry you. Therefore it would make her happy."

"I see. . . . " But Norman didn't see. As usual, he felt at such a disadvantage with this boy.

"So I'll give you my permission if you promise something."

"What?"

"My mother has been so unhappy for such a long time. She's a person who wants to laugh, and she hasn't had much of a chance to laugh for years, not since my father got sick. So you've got to promise to take her to lots of places, and have a lot of parties here at the house. And you've got to take her to Europe, too. She went to Europe once before she got married, and she's always wanted to go back. So you've got to promise to take her to Europe."

"Now see here, boy, this will all take money."

"But you'll have lots of money after you marry my mother."

The boy was still looking at him, his face intent and serious, his eyes guileless. But then how could you tell they were guileless, when he had eyes like that, blue eyes just like his mother's? Damn it all, what did the boy know?

No . . . no . . . he mustn't go into that again. If Euin knew anything about the murder, he had had his chance to say so. So he didn't know.

"Uncle Norman, will you make my mother laugh and be happy?"

"Well naturally, I intend to . . . "

"And you'll go out to places, and have parties, and take her to Europe?"

"Of course."

"Then you have my permission to marry her."

"Thank you." Weakly, confused, Norman stumbled to the door, wanting only to escape from the boy's presence.

But at the threshold the youthful, not yet fully mature voice stopped him. "One more thing, Uncle Norman."

He turned. The boy had the book open in his lap and was abstractedly flipping the pages.

"What is it, Euin?"

"I should like to go to military school next year. I haven't decided which one, but I'll let you know."

"Military school?"

"Yes, you don't want me hanging around here, do you? Two's company, but three's a crowd, they say. And besides, everything would be spoiled for you, now that you know for sure that I'm not very fond of you."

Norman stared, but the boy had already gone back to reading the book. Norman tried to think of something to say. But he couldn't think of anything at all. So he opened the door and went out, and shut the door quietly behind him.

Norman should have enjoyed his European honeymoon. He'd never been abroad before, and he had with him the bride of his heart's choice.

But there were drawbacks. In 1947 the continent was still digging out from bomb rubble and there was rationing of all sorts. Clare enjoyed herself immensely, always looking for something she remembered and discovering whether it was intact, changed, or ruined. It was a kind of game with her. But to Norman the trip was one long inconvenience.

Even Clare was something of a disappointment. He couldn't analyze exactly why, though he tried. He'd been in love with her, wanted her, for seventeen years. That waiting period should have sharpened his appetite. But perhaps he had anticipated too long, and no woman could have fulfilled his expectations. Then, too, he had met Clare when she was twenty. She was thirty-seven now. Still beautiful, of course. But there was no doubt, he told himself, that Arnold had had Clare's best years.

Then at times his conscience would seem to awaken, and he would feel that everything was being spoiled—being the master of a small fortune and of a beautiful woman—by the fact that he'd committed a murder. At these times, he would suffer a day of deep gloom until his mind could commence to rationalize again that it hadn't been a murder he'd done, but a mercy killing.

But he suffered his blackest despair when he thought of Euin. It was all Euin's fault. He, Norman, did not really lack desire for Clare, nor was he being terribly gnawed at by the worm of conscience. The whole trouble was that his new possessions, his money and his wife, were not secure so long as Euin held the secret of how he'd acquired those possessions.

Why doesn't the boy speak up? He knows I'm guilty of murder. That's what gives him his superior attitude with me. That's why he knows he can have his own way with me. "Take my mother to Europe, and send me to a military school." It was nothing short of blackmail. So he knows. I know that he knows. *But what is he waiting for?*

It was in Venice, riding in a gondola—with the gondolier serenading Clare in incomprehensible Italian, and with Clare reclining at the far end of the boat gazing up at the Mediterranean moon—that Norman Landers decided he would have to commit another murder.

But murdering a cripple in his bed is one thing, and disposing of a healthy, intelligent, suspicious, alert young boy is quite another. Norman Landers entered a period of frustration more intense than he'd ever experienced while Clare was Arnold's wife or while he was waiting for Arnold to die.

The appropriate time, Norman figured, would be the summer vacation, when Euin returned from school. He had several projects in mind. There would be the shooting accident when he and Euin went out hunting together. Or there would be the accidental drowning when he and Euin went boating. Or there would be the fall down the nice cliff he'd selected when he and Euin tramped off together for a hike in the woods.

Of course, none of these plans ever came to fruition. Their weakness lay in the fact that each plan demanded conviviality and comradeship between the man and the boy.

"Why do you keep pestering me, Uncle Norman?" the boy asked one day.

"Am I pestering you?"

"Yes, you are. Always asking me to go somewhere with you."

"I simply thought we should become better companions."

"But I thought we'd agreed, Uncle Norman, that I don't like you."

Enraged, Norman wanted to strike the boy, but he held back just in time. Fourteen, Euin was nearly as tall as Norman himself, becoming well-muscled, and was obviously athletic and in good condition. The outcome of any physical encounter would be at least doubtful.

In fact, Norman suddenly reflected in horror, so would the outcome be of any attempted drowning or falling accident. He was lucky that he hadn't tried either of those with the boy.

"You're not looking well, Uncle Norman," Euin was remarking.

"I feel fine," Norman lied.

"You're dissipating at Mother's parties, that's what you're doing."

"Damn those parties!" Norman exclaimed in a sudden outburst of anger.

"What did you say, Uncle?"

"I said, damn those parties!"

"Don't you like them?"

"No, I don't. . . ."

"But they make Mother very happy, don't they?"

"Oh, she's very pleased . . . "

"Well, that's the important thing, isn't it? We both want to see Mother happy, don't we, Uncle Norman?"

They confronted each other for a moment. The boy's eyes were so blue, so innocent. And yet the secret was there, somewhere, perhaps in his smile—a smile that was just barely a smile, just the slightest crease at one corner of the boy's full, sensual mouth.

During the ensuing years, Norman Landers attempted murder a number of times. Not with bloody violent weapons such as a gun, or a knife, or an axe, for Norman was not a violent man. Nor by the only slightly less violent methods of accidental death, which he had once contemplated but which were no longer practical. Neither by the more devious, more subtle means of poison, which he had once employed successfully. There had been the opportunity for that with Euin's father, but there was none with Euin himself. Although Norman did consider once inducing ptomaine poisoning with spoiled fish or something. The only trouble was he couldn't devise how he could get Euin to eat the fish and not have to eat the fish himself.

No, the method he finally chose was the most subtle, the most devious, and the safest. Also, unfortunately, it depended on luck. His good luck and Euin's bad.

For the boy's fifteenth birthday, Norman gave him a motorbike. It was a shiny, racy job that would capture any youngster whether he harbored any secrets about a murder or not.

"This is a pretty fast machine," the salesman said. "It'll do a hundred easily. Would you like a governor installed?"

"We'll bring it back later for that," Norman answered. "But I've got to take the bike along right now. It's a present, you see . . . "

When the boy was sixteen, and so could qualify for a driver's license, his Uncle Norman bought him a car. Actually it wasn't just a car. It was an imported sports model.

"I'll bet this is faster than my old bike," Euin observed delightedly.

"It's much faster," Norman assured him.

At seventeen, when he was entering an Eastern university which boasted an Alpine Club, the boy received a complete skiing and mountain-climbing outfit.

At eighteen, he switched to an oceanside university and got a speedboat as a present. He stayed at that school and at nineteen received skin-diving equipment.

Then just before Euin was twenty, Norman's diligence and persistence were almost rewarded. But the accident was only a minor one. The car was pretty thoroughly damaged, but the driver was unscratched. So on his twentieth birthday, Euin received a newer, faster car.

And some advice. "After an accident, my boy," Euin was told, "you've got to start driving again immediately. Otherwise you'll build up a phobia and you can never bring yourself to drive again."

At twenty-one, the boy graduated to an airplane, complete with a set of flying lessons.

But Euin endured all these hazards, any one of which would easily have killed Norman. Because Norman was such an ordinary man, full of fears, so conscious of danger that he saw it everywhere. After all, he had murdered Arnold only because the opportunity had been so obvious, the doing so easy, and the risk so small. When it came right down to it, Norman wasn't really a first-class murderer.

But Euin Landers endured because he was so like his mother. He preferred to live life. She had managed to be happy without much help from a husband, and Euin had grown up fatherless but splendidly.

And Norman had grown old before his time. There'd been his grisly fear of Euin, and his frustrated attempts to rid himself of the tormentor. Then there had been his marriage with Clare, their incompatibility. Now finally there was the worry about money.

All of these difficulties which plagued him reached sort of a climax when Euin fell in love with Della Sherman.

In the business of love and marriage, Euin ran true to form also, following rather faithfully in his mother's footsteps. Della Sherman was not exactly Euin's type, but she was not unattractive. Mainly, however, she was wealthy. Much wealthier, in fact, than Arnold Landers had been when Clare married him. But there'd been a lot of inflation in the intervening time.

Clare, now a comely matron in her forties and finally inclined to stoutness, plunged into the problem of Euin's pursuit and courtship of Della with unflagging vigor. And she quickly alerted Norman to his duties.

"It's a wonderful opportunity for Euin," she explained. "He'll be set for life once he marries Della. But we've got to launch him, darling, we've got to launch him."

"What does that mean," Norman asked fearfully.

"It means we have to impress the Shermans. We can't let them think that Euin is a fortune-hunter, that their Della is marrying a poor boy."

"And what does that mean, Clare?"

"We must begin to entertain more," she said. She waltzed around the room—without Norman, of course—in a frenzy of anticipation. "First it will mean redoing the house right away, so we can have the Shermans over. And then some parties. Not the little parties we've been having, darling. But on a lavish scale."

"Clare . . . " he protested.

Of course it didn't do any good to protest. They redid the house and they had the parties. So many of them that Norman lost count.

And anyway, for him they were all the same. They had hired a butler, and on the evenings of the parties the catering service sent in extra waiters, but there was always something for him to do. An extra plate of hors d'oeuvres to be passed around, or some dowager to fetch a drink for, somebody's car to be moved in the drive for somebody else to get out, or a mad dash down the highway in search of more ice cubes. Clare's idea of being a hostess was to be always dancing, as if she were the guest of honor. He didn't care much, because if he'd had to dance with her, it would have been even more fatiguing than the errands he constantly had to run.

It was at one of those parties—the only one in Norman's memory distinguishable from the others—that Clare delivered the final blow. She found him in the kitchen and began dragging him out to the living room. As they went, she whispered furiously into his ear.

"Euin's going to make a surprise announcement of the engagement," she said.

"Who will it surprise?" he wondered wearily.

"And I want to do something," Clare continued rapidly, "to make sure that the Shermans don't raise any objections. I want to announce that we're going to give Euin a house as a wedding present."

He stopped in the middle of the crowded room and challenged her in a low voice. "What house?"

"Euin and I have picked it out already. It's going up right now on an exclusive acre. And it's only sixty thousand. . . . "

"Sixty thousand!" He thought he was going to faint.

"That's all, darling. But remember, Euin is marrying into millions."

"But, Clare, we don't have sixty thousand."

"Yes, we do, darling. I've mortgaged this house."

In June, Euin Landers and Della Sherman were married with elaborate spectacle, and departed on a round-the-world honeymoon. In August, Clare Landers, having lived life to the fullest, saw fit to have a heart attack and die. Euin and Della flew home hurriedly from Tahiti. Euin arranged a most lavish funeral.

They talked together for the last time on the evening after that funeral. There'd been other people around during the day, relatives, friends, sympathizers—all the old party-goers had come to Clare's last rites—but now in the evening there were only the two of them left. They wandered into the library together.

"Drink, Uncle Norman?" Euin asked.

Norman had never become accustomed to the habit of drinking, but now he said, "Yes, I think I will."

Euin mixed a pair of strong highballs, and they sipped them facing each other from opposite sides of the fireplace. It was a chilly evening, but there was no fire burning. There were no servants to light one. Probably there was no wood anyway.

"Well, here's to Mother," Euin said as he raised his glass.

They drank together. Then Norman said, "That's a queer thing, to drink a toast to a person who's dead."

"Well, let's put it another way then. Let's drink to the happy reunion of my mother and my father."

Norman hesitated only for a second before he lifted his glass and drank again. "Yes, let it be a happy one," he said.

"I think it will be." Euin's gaze was very direct now. "After all, my mother has had a happy life. That will have pleased my father."

"I hope so." Norman drank more swiftly.

"And all thanks to you."

Norman tried to meet the younger man's gaze, failed, and turned away. "Oh, I don't know that I contributed so much," he said.

"Oh, you did, Uncle Norman. More than you realize. You made your first contribution, remember, when you poisoned my father."

There was a heavy silence in the room, punctuated finally by Norman's deep sigh. A sigh of relief.

"So you knew," he said.

"Of course I knew."

"I always thought you did. But the thing that puzzled me was your silence. Why didn't you tell anybody?"

"You haven't guessed why?"

"No, I'm afraid I haven't." He looked pleadingly across at Euin, but he found no responding emotion there. Euin was wearing the same old blank expression that he'd worn at so many of their earlier encounters.

"Well, if you'll remember, Uncle Norman, I was with my father when he died."

"Yes, I remember."

"And we had a long talk."

"Yes, you said you talked about things that were just between the two of you. I remember your saying that so well."

"I think I can reveal our secret now, Uncle Norman."

"I should like to know it."

"To begin with, though I lied about this to the police, my father did tell me that he wanted to die. He said that you had suggested suicide to him, and he hadn't had the courage for it. So he leaned on your courage. He was actually glad you murdered him, Uncle Norman."

Norman Landers listened silently. Even his drink, which he had needed for courage, sat forgotten beside him.

"My father told me he was glad to be dying. Life was no longer of any use to him and he could be nothing but a burden to his wife and son. The fact that his dear and trusted cousin had murdered him, however, posed a problem."

Euin paused, drained his glass, lit a cigarette. He went through these motions, it seemed, with deliberate slowness, as if to irritate his single listener.

"The revelation of murder would, of course, properly punish the murderer. But unfortunately it would also punish the wife and son. Neither could ever escape the notoriety of a murder. Suicide, my father felt—at least suicide under circumstances that certainly justified it—was a preferable stigma."

"Your father told you all this?" Norman interrupted wonderingly. "You were only a boy."

"I was twelve years old. I understood it pretty well then. But as the years passed, I understood it better. My father was right. If we had exposed you as a murderer, certainly Mother wouldn't have had a happy life afterwards, and I wouldn't be married to Della Sherman today."

Norman sighed again. "True," he said thoughtfully.

"My father wanted to protect us above all," Euin said. "And he wanted my mother to be happy too. She needed someone to watch out for her. She was a pretty carefree sort. My father understood that. 'When I'm dead,' my father explained, 'Lord knows what silly thing Clare is apt to do. She really needs a solid sort like old Norm.' I objected to that. The idea of my father's murderer marrying my mother appalled me. But my father made me promise. 'See that your mother marries Uncle Norman,' he said. And I've got to admit it now, Uncle Norman, that he was right. If my mother hadn't been respectably married to you, she might have gotten into trouble. So I suppose I must thank you for that."

Norman listened numbly. Euin's voice seemed to be coming from far off.

" 'But see to it,' my father cautioned me, 'that he treats her right. That she lives her way, not his. Your mother has to have her good times, remember. And also see to it that you and your mother get the good out of my money. Don't let old Norm profit too much out of this affair.' Well, I guess I've obeyed my father pretty well there too, haven't I, Uncle Norman? My mother had her good times, I got my education, those expensive toys you hoped I'd kill myself with, and now as a matter of fact, I'm set for life. It has worked out pretty neatly, I think. You've served your purpose, Uncle Norman. Mother is dead, I'm fixed up, and you don't have a penny."

Euin paused to flick his burned-out cigarette into the yawning blackness of the empty fireplace. Then he stood up, straightening his well-cut, black funeral suit.

"I'd better be going," he announced. "You've served your time, Uncle. You committed a crime, and you've served your sentence. You came into this prison without a cent and you're leaving it without a cent. But you've had your board and room in the meantime. I suppose I shouldn't begrudge you that."

Norman didn't rise. "This is good-bye then?" he asked.

"This is good-bye, Uncle."

"What is going to happen to me?"

"I don't really care. In fact, I hope you starve."

Norman Landers gazed into the dead fireplace. His mind was moving sluggishly. He didn't want to starve. "After all I've done for you and your mother . . . and your father too, for that matter," he said piteously.

He heard rather than saw Euin's movement toward the door. Then just before those footsteps crossed the threshold, he spoke.

"Euin!"

"Yes, Uncle?"

"If I'm starving, if I have no roof over my head, I'll have just one recourse. To go to the police and tell them it was I who murdered Arnold Landers."

"Uncle . . . "

"And I wonder what those fine Shermans would think of that?"

There was a long silence.

Then, "What do you want, Uncle Norman?"

Norman spoke slowly. There was a book at his elbow. He took the book into his lap and began to flip the pages abstractedly as he spoke. "First of all, I want to make one thing clear. I don't particularly like you, Nephew. Secondly, I don't want any parties. I want to be left strictly alone. But I want a nice comfortable house and I want a bit of money. Let's see . . . about no, maybe a little more than that. . . . "

DEAD DRUNK Arthur Porges

IT TAKES A LOT to stump an experienced pathologist, and even more to surprise him. Nor will any findings, no matter how grotesque, shock a man familiar with every possible use and abuse of the body.

But some weeks ago I was in at the finish of a case that made me dig deeper than is necessary in most of them, and had me tangled up in my own emotions like a kitten with a ball of yarn.

It was one of Lieutenant Ader's headaches. He and I have worked together, informally, for a number of years. Although I'm not officially connected with the Norfolk City Police, Pasteur Hospital is the only one around with a full-time pathologist on the staff. That's me—Dr. Joel Hoffman, middle-aged, unmarried—possibly because of my dedication to my work. And since the nearest adequate crime lab is a hundred and fifty miles away, Ader calls on me occasionally to carry out autopsies and other tests which the local coroner—a political hack—is unable to handle properly.

The case really began fifteen months ago, and oddly enough I was there, although without any idea of the ramifications to come later. At that time, the lieutenant was driving us back from a stabbing at the south end of town:

a simple matter, with no subtleties, consisting of a steak knife driven into a lung. But on the way home, we heard a radio call about a traffic accident not too far off, and Ader decided to have a look. It never does any harm to barge in on your subordinates by surprise now and then; keeps them on their toes, Ader feels.

It turned out to be a typical and infuriating example of the genus legal murder. We found a huge garish convertible, a shaky driver, and a dazed woman crouching over the body of her child, a boy about eight.

As we pulled up, the man responsible for the tragedy was protesting to all and sundry, but especially to the pair of stonyfaced officers from the prowl car.

"I'm not drunk," he insisted, his voice only slightly thick. "It's my diabetes; I need insulin. Sure, I had a couple, but I'm quite sober."

The man reeked of alcohol, but his actions were not those of a drunk. This is a familiar phenomenon. The shock of the accident had blasted the maggots from his nervous system, so that to the casual observer, he seemed in full command of himself.

I was busy with the child. There wasn't a hope. He died before the ambulance got there five minutes later. The mother, smartly dressed and attractive, knelt there pale and rigid, as if in a trance. It was that dangerous state before the blessed release of tears.

I never did learn the details of the accident. Apparently, mother and son, the latter leading a puppy, were waiting at the crosswalk, when the animal got away. Before the woman could stop him, the child had scampered into the street. He should have been safe in the cross-walk in any circumstances; the law is strict about that; but the car was moving too fast, and its driver was drunk. An old story.

Ader watched the interns put the pathetic little body into the ambulance. The heavy muscles of his jaw corded.

"I know this murderer and his convertible," Ader told me in a gritty voice. "He was sure to kill somebody sooner or later. A worthless guy if ever there was one. I wish we could nail him this time."

I took a good look at the man. Plump, expensively dressed, well tanned, sun-lamp style, not the kind you get out in the air. He had a jowly face with bags under the eyes. His earlier paleness was gone, but he seemed nervous, and yet arrogant, too, as if he anticipated a punch in the nose, and was ready to yell police brutality.

"You can't blame a man for diabetic coma, Lieutenant," he said defiantly. "You've tried it before, and the jury didn't buy any. I'm Gordon Vance Whitman, remember, not some scared, friendless punk you can frame."

"You're drunk," Ader said. "And you forgot the 'third' at the end of your distinguished name."

"Like hell I am. Diabetic coma." There was a sly glint in his small eyes.

I glanced at the lieutenant. He shrugged in disgust.

"We've had this guy up several times for drunk driving; nobody was killed before—just maimed. He has diabetes, all right; and the symptoms are rather similar, as you know. A jury isn't competent to assess the difference, not with a gaggle of high-priced lawyers working on them."

"The juries are fine," Whitman grinned, swaying a little. "All I need is a pill. With deliberate ostentation he pulled a vial from one pocket, opened it, and popped a tablet into his mouth. I spotted the label; the stuff was one of those new drugs which, for people over forty, takes the place of insulin. "Just a matter of excess blood sugar," he said, making sure the scene went on record.

"You don't seem much concerned about the child you killed," I told him, feeling a strong urge to mash a handful of knuckles against his beautifully capped teeth.

"Naturally, I'm very sorry," he replied in a solemn voice. "But it wasn't my fault; the kid ran out after that fool pup all of a sudden."

"That's no excuse," Ader snapped. "If you hadn't been soused and speeding, you could have stopped in plenty of time. You hit him in a cross walk."

"If I *was* going too fast," Whitman explained, "it happened after the coma dazed me. I blanked out for a minute and may have stepped on the gas."

"You can at least see that he never drives again," I reminded Ader.

"Yeah," he said wearily. "That'll cheer the parents no end. You don't know the half of it, son. Let's get out of here: Briggs and Gerber can handle the details."

"Wait a minute," I said. "What about her?"

Ader jumped, as though startled. "You're right. I'm an idiot."

We both looked at the woman. She was still crouched there, but now she was cradling the puppy in her arms. A low, pathetic moaning came from her throat, and the little animal, tightly gripped and unhappy, joined in with a shrill whimper.

"Look," Ader said. "You and Briggs take her home in the cruiser. Get her husband, and call the family doctor."

It seemed a good idea. I managed to get her on her feet, and over to the police car. Briggs climbed in, and we were off. The low moaning became louder; suddenly she was weeping with passionate intensity. That was all to the good, though there are limits.

It's been at least ten years since I had a patient to treat. All of mine are just bodies to be studied. Nevertheless, I always carry a minimum emergency kit, and it came in handy now. I had a devil of a time, but finally managed to give her a sedative. I'll never forget that ride: the woman, her dainty dress all smeared from the gutter; her carefully made-up face a wild mask of grief; and that pitiful puppy's whimpering, incessant and at times shrill.

Twice the woman pulled away from me and tried to jump out of the moving car. "I want to go back!" she cried. "Where did they take Derry? Let me go; let me go!"

Well, we got her home at last, and called her husband, a college professor. He picked up the family doctor on the way, and I was relieved from duty. Briggs dropped me off at the hospital, where I found hours of work already piled up. Yet busy as I was, I couldn't get the incident off my mind. Do doctors ever get used to that sort of thing? I wondered. More than ever, I felt I'd been wise in avoiding general practice. It was too easy to get involved. For days I winced every time I thought of that poor woman and her loss.

Some time later, Ader gave me the whole sad story of Gordon Vance Whitman III. This character was a playboy of fifty plus and almost as many millions. One of the most sued people in the country. He'd never been any good, and the chief thing of interest about him was the foresight of his father, a canny old pirate of an earlier generation, when financial morals were even lower than now. He had put the boy's inheritance in the form of an unbreakable trust, of which Gordon enjoyed only the income. Such arrangements, which unfairly protect irresponsibles like Whitman against legitimate claims, are barred in most states, but not, alas, in mine. The income, of course, was enormous by ordinary standards, and cleverly designed to make tracing and attaching any portion of it as tricky as legally possible.

Whitman had married the usual series of showgirls, all of whom were collecting large slices of his assorted dividends; but other judgments, totaling millions, were unenforceable because of the machinations of the late Whitman, Senior.

In short, Ader saw little hope of convicting Whitman this time either.

Well, I was too busy to keep track of one more social injustice—the needless death of a child—among many. I seem to recall that Whitman's license was revoked for a long time, and another large judgment added to the list. He beat the drunk charge, since blood tests are barred here. The old diabetes story was good again. As for transportation, there are chauffeurs available for a price, and after enough high-toned specialists had testified that his diabetes was under control, this model citizen may even have recovered his maiming rights.

Occasionally I saw an item about him—he was always

news. Another marriage, a starlet this time. Apparently he favored petite redheads; this was the fourth to become Mrs. Whitman.

"A few more marriages," Ader remarked sourly once, "and maybe the guy'll be too worn out to drive around killing children!"

The accident happened over a year ago, and seemed to be past history, but last month saw a new phase of the Whitman story, and it was a lulu.

Ader phoned me late on a Tuesday afternoon. The body of a man had just been found inside a locked, third-floor apartment. No marks of violence; no sign of any other party's having been present, even. The victim had apparently enjoyed a lone binge behind a bolted door. He had then stretched out on the divan, and instead of awakening with a size-twelve head and lepidoptera in his stomach, never came to at all.

"And the dear departed," Ader told me with ghoulish satisfaction, "is none other than our old friend, Gordon Vance Whitman III."

"Good," I remarked. "But where do I fit in?"

"We have a curious policy here at headquarters. We'd like to know what this crumb died of."

"You'd better take the usual pictures, and then bring me the body," I told him. "I can't possibly leave the hospital today. In any case, it certainly sounds like a stroke or coronary."

"Very likely," Ader agreed. "But I have an instinct in these matters, and let's be sure, okay?"

"Fair enough. Bring me the remains, and I'll do the pm this evening."

At that stage, of course, there was no indication of murder, what with the locked door and all. There aren't many John Dickson Carr puzzles in real life.

The police brought me the body about five, and I got all the details and photos. It was a matter of luck that Whitman had been found so promptly. One of his numerous lady friends, unable to rouse him by leaning on the buzzer, had finally called the manager, who in turn notified the police. They had broken in, seen that the man was dead, and now it was up to me. We all expected that the cause of death was something quick, massive, and natural. I would have bet on it myself. Hence my first real surprise in years.

Now, an autopsy, when properly done, is a long and involved chore. The "gross" part, actually carried out on the table, is almost identical with a series of major operations, and performed with the same care and precision as if the person were still alive and under anaesthesia. No sloppy hacking will do; the job takes from three to six hours with a conscientious pathologist. The microscopic phase, completed in the laboratory, may go on for weeks, and could include work in chemistry, bacteriology, toxicology, and any other speciality you'd care to name.

My preliminary examination seemed to confirm the existence of some sort of respiratory failure, for the face was gray and the lips bluish—a condition called cyanosis. Nevertheless, there is a standard routine for a postmortem, so I began with the skull. The brain tissue was quite normal; no sign of a bloodclot there, which ruled out one kind of stroke.

Next, working by the book, I explored the chest cavity, and found pay dirt immediately. The appearance of the lungs: the edema and signs of severe irritation, caught my eye at once. I bent over for a better look with a 3X magnifier, and as my face came close, noted an odd odor—the faint, musty smell of new-mown hay, along with the sharper, unmistakable reek of hydrochloric acid.

It was a clue I might easily have missed. That would have meant many hours of lab work to discover the obvious. You see, nobody who served in the Army would forget that scent of moldy hay. In the early months of 1942, when gas warfare seemed highly probable, every soldier, and particularly those of us in the Medical Corps, was taught to recognize the main types of poison gas. This unique smell meant phosgene, a deadly stuff invented during World War I. A few good whiffs, and the victim, beyond a little coughing and chest congestion, might go about his business unworried, only to collapse and die later, without warning. It's tricky and variable, forming hydrochloric acid in the lungs. Real nasty, that vapor.

I told you it was a puzzler—a man dead of phosgene in a locked room. The case was no longer one of death by natural causes or accident—not with the victim's lungs full of poison gas.

Now don't misunderstand me; I'm a pathologist, not a detective. Theoretically, when I completed the rest of the autopsy, my job was done. But when something this intriguing comes along, which is seldom, and they can spare me at the hospital, I like to tag along with the lieutenant. Sometimes I've been helpful; at worst, I'm a useful sounding board.

Well, he took me to the apartment, where I got another jolt. I'd assumed, reasonably enough, that somebody had pumped phosgene into the room; there didn't seem to be any other explanation. But I was wrong. A few simple tests showed that no such wholesale release of gas had occurred. Fantastic as it seemed, the stuff must have been introduced directly into the man's lungs—and only there. That seemed to imply a tank of phosgene, along with a tube or mask. It was a sticker, all right.

But Ader skipped that point for the moment. Instead we concentrated on the source, thinking that would be easier. You don't just pick up a tank of war gas at the corner drugstore. It's not too hard to make a little of it, chemically, but not in any form that would permit it being pumped into a person's lungs.

The lieutenant checked all the nearby Army camps. We weren't too surprised to find that none of them stocked the stuff. Gas warfare is nearly passé. All they had were those recognition kits which teach rookies the characteristic odors. Harmless samples. The one big chemical-warfare depot was able to state positively that no phosgene—stored in big tanks—was missing.

That left the question of motive, which gave us both a

grim chuckle. It was obvious that Gordon Vance Whitman III had plenty of enemies. Not so many as the late Hitler, maybe, but quite a few.

The money angle was a flop. Whitman had no heirs. In the event of his death, the huge trust became a sort of foundation like the Ford or Rockefeller setup. Which meant that none of those judgments would be any better than they were now—in short, useless to the litigants.

Well, police work is mostly tiresome routine. Somebody had murdered, and how we still didn't know, the late Mr. Whitman. Therefore it was a matter of motive. Ader and his staff had to check out a list of more than twenty prime suspects, all people with good reasons for hating the victim. I withdrew from that part of the case; they were yelling for me at the hospital anyway. Instead, I continued to ponder the phosgene problem. I kept gnawing at it during the weeks Ader's crew was struggling with the leg-work.

Their efforts finally paid off. Everybody was eliminated from the list, but one woman. She was definitely It. Oddly enough, the lieutenant hadn't felt strongly about including her at the start; it was almost certain, he thought, that she had no connection with the case. But the principles of sound police work sink deep into a competent officer, and her name was added to the others. You see, she was merely the maid who cleaned the hallways and did similar odd jobs. The apartments themselves were the problem of the tenants.

She called herself Mrs. Talbot, but the first thorough check soon revealed that her right name was Eleanor Oldenburger. A college graduate, the widow of a distinguished professor, she had recently suffered a complete nervous collapse. She had taken this job a few weeks after leaving the hospital. On the off chance that her arriving at this particular building might be significant, Ader looked for a connection between Whitman and her. It didn't take long to find one. If anybody had a good reason to loathe the late playboy, Mrs. Oldenburger qualified in spades. We were brought back fifteen months to the killing of that little boy. His name was Derry, and he was the Oldenburgers' only child. Loss of the boy had undoubtedly hastened the professor's death. Their small amount of insurance went for the widow's medical expenses—nervous breakdowns come high. A damage suit initiated by the professor before his death had resulted in a judgment of $300,000, but there were dozens of others ahead of it, all uncollectible.

When Ader told me all this, I looked him in the eye, and said, "If she did kill him, more power to her. Why not drop the case now?"

He didn't lower his own stare for a moment.

"I'm a police officer. I can't do that. I'm no judge; you know that." A crooked little smile touched his lips. "I certainly want to know *how* she managed it, but if there isn't enough evidence to make a case, I won't be heartbroken." He paused. "Husband, child—all lost because of that stinker. You can't really blame her."

"What's she like?" I asked him.

"You saw her. Woman in her forties, I'd say. So far, I've seen her only at work, not in her home, in those shapeless things maids wear for dirty jobs. I've a hunch it was mostly protective coloration. I seem to remember a pair of electric-blue eyes that didn't fit a common drudge at all. But I'm about to visit her at home. Why not come along?"

I jumped at the chance. Although I was no nearer to a solution of the phosgene puzzle, the woman began to interest me for herself. Whatever her plan, it showed a cool, keen intelligence, as well as the ruthless judgment of a Minerva.

She lived in a tiny but immaculate apartment in Orange Grove. I saw Ader blink at the sight of her. She wore well-tailored slacks of gray material, and a pale-blue blouse; they emphasized a slender, but rounded figure that suggested twenty-five rather than forty-five. Her hair was of the sort Holmes called "positive blonde," that is, fair, but with highlights and subtle colors. She seemed quite relaxed.

With almost insolent coolness, she insisted on our having martinis. When we were settled with ours, she curled up catlike on a big sofa and gave us a faint smile.

"Let the inquisition begin," she said lightly. On the surface she was hard, cold, and callous. As a doctor, trained to study people behind their pathetic facades, I knew that her nerves were stretched to an unbearable tension, that she was on the knife-edge of hysteria.

Ader was brusque. I think he too sensed her delicate balance and hoped to break her down.

"Why didn't you tell us your real name?"

Her smile deepened.

"Come, Lieutenant. I was taking a menial job, under very distressing circumstances. Why should I parade my identity as a fallen woman?"

"You deliberately picked that building to work in. The manager testified that you phoned her repeatedly. Why did it have to be there? Wasn't it so you could get at Whitman?"

"You know, of course," she reminded him sweetly, "that I needn't answer any of these questions without a lawyer. But I've nothing to hide. I liked the location; as you see, it's near this apartment. I could walk; I'm too nervous these days to drive, and can't afford a car, anyway. And what makes you think I'd want to kill Whitman?"

"Look, Mrs. Oldenburger," Ader said. "We know about Derry. In case you've forgotten, Dr. Hoffman and I happened to be on the spot just after that swine, Whitman—"

She was deathly pale now, but interrupted him in an even voice.

"You agree, then, that he was a swine."

"Of course. I sympathize with you in every way. But I can't condone murder."

"Neither can you prove it," she flashed. "I understand his apartment was bolted inside."

"The transom was partly open. Isn't it true that you use a small ladder to clean woodwork in the halls?"

"Yes. I'm only five feet six, you see."

"Were you using it that day?"

"Yes. Did I crawl through the transom and kill Whitman?"

Ader frowned. "No, it's too small even for you. I measured it."

She gave him a look of mock consternation. "Oh, dear. And me bragging about my slender build."

"We don't know how you did it—yet. But obviously you found out where he lived, and wangled this job as a maid. Somehow you managed to fill his lungs with poison gas—phosgene, to be exact. It's only a matter of time until we discover the method."

She raised her carefully penciled brows, and squirmed deeper into the soft cushions. She seemed perfectly relaxed, but I could see a significantly throbbing vein by one ear.

"Phosgene? I doubt if I could spell it, in spite of my general chemistry in college. As for that job, I had a complete breakdown. Probably you know all about that, too. For weeks I was catatonic. When I recovered, any mental effort was still impossible. I had to find some simple physical work. That's all there is to it. I'm no scientific genius to make poison gas and get it into a locked room."

"What makes you think it had to be made?" Ader snapped. "Why not bought?"

She tightened visibly, aware of her mistake.

"Can you go out and buy poison gas?" she asked brightly. "I wouldn't know. But, in any case, gentlemen, it's getting late, and if you don't mind . . . "

We left then; there wasn't much else to do. She was under a terrific strain, but wouldn't crack. Yet I felt sure reaction and regrets were inevitable. And I didn't like the prospect.

But intellectual curiosity is a passion with me, so I couldn't quit. And the next day I made my first real advance. I placed the name Oldenburger. Surely I had seen some of his articles in the past. What had they covered?

Then it came to me; the man had been a top physiological chemist, often consulted by the big poison centers.

I got in touch with the nearest one immediately, with highly significant results. The puzzle was solved now, except for one small item. Ader supplied that, but didn't know it. It was the first time I held out on him. I merely asked for a list of cleaning agents available to the maids in Whitman's building. Among them, sure enough, was carbon tetrachloride, kept on hand to remove spots from upholstery. I decided to pay Mrs. Oldenburger a visit on my own.

This time she wore a simple dress, the kind that is tasteful-expensive-simple, if you know what I mean. It confirmed my suspicion that she was far from broke, and didn't actually need a job as maid.

Seeing her again, I realized what an attractive woman she really was. Without Ader there, she seemed to be more natural. As I'd suspected, the hardness and diamond sparkle had been at least partially assumed before—a shield.

My emotions were clawing me. I meant to prove I knew the solution, but after that—well, the way wasn't clear at all.

I accepted a drink, and for some minutes we made small talk. I began to lose hope of getting through, because the woman was at peace with herself. Apparently her conscience had been stilled; perhaps she had finally rationalized the murder to the point of feeling no guilt.

Relaxed and warm, she had that rare facility of withholding the best part of her considerable beauty, and then in a dazzling stroke, flashing it like a weapon. I had no defense against it and didn't seem to want one.

The small talk had to end sometime. I took the plunge.

"I know exactly how you did it," I told her.

A slight shadow passed over her face.

"I was more afraid of you than of the officer," she said. "My husband mentioned your work occasionally. A new test for morphine poisoning, I believe."

I may have blushed; this was, naturally, hardly what I expected as a counter.

"Thank you. And I know about Professor Oldenburger. He had a very intriguing case once at the poison center. Maybe he discussed it with you. Whitman's addiction to liquor was the key. It's an odd fact of chemistry that if a man with plenty of alcohol in his system gets a few whiffs of carbon tetrachloride, the two compounds unite in the blood to form phosgene, one of the deadliest of the early war gases. Now I believe you soaked a rag in the spot remover, and using a mop handle or something, reached through the transom to hold the cloth over Whitman's nose and mouth. With the ladder it was a cinch. Two or three minutes would be enough time. If anybody had appeared, you could have pulled away from the transom and busied yourself with the moldings. Besides, who knows better than a maid how deserted those apartments are by day?" I looked at her pale, composed face. "Am I right? There are no witnesses here, so why not admit it?"

She sat there, a fragile figure, with that odd air of repose, and my heart went out to her.

"Not quite," she said shakily. "I used a fishing rod. Rufus —my husband—was a great one for trout. It was the rod," she added, with a catch in her voice, "he taught Derry on." She turned her head away for a moment.

"It's hardly a case to stand up in court," I told her. "I doubt if any jury—"

"No," she said passionately. "You mustn't say that. I've been mad, distracted. It was a terrible thing. I have nightmares when I think of putting that awful rag—a sleeping man, helpless . . . " She straightened in the chair. "I've signed a confession. I want you to call Lieutenant Ader."

To my surprise, I found myself protesting. The words came in a wild flood. I told her without my testimony, there was no case; that I wouldn't go to court. That Ader didn't know about the spot remover. She smiled as if I were a child.

She pled guilty, but by law a trial is still possible. I got the best lawyer in the state. I was now convinced she had been temporarily insane, and that was the line we held. The jury wouldn't convict.

During the long weeks of legal maneuvering, we grew closer together. I never dreamed I'd marry a murderess, but, as I said at the start, it's not easy to shock a pathologist.

THE LAST AUTOPSY Bryce Walton

DOC CROWELL sat up all of that night with Old Nancy
Stokes out by Reeve's Mill, soothing her recurrent fever
and listening patiently to stories of the Civil War he had
heard often before. He got back to his home in Cypressville
at sunup and managed to grab the phone in the parlor halfway through its first ring. He didn't want it to wake his
wife before he could get out of the house once again.

He chuckled wearily as he lifted the receiver, sure that
it would be Pete Hines calling about his wife, Hanna, who
was about due again. It would be the twelfth little Hines
that Doc Crowell had brought into an unsuspecting world,
and Pete still owed him for the last five deliveries. Pete was
quite a con-man even for Cypressville. He always planned
his wife's deliveries to time up with those of his Guernsey
cow, so that Doc Crowell would have to deliver a calf, too,
thereby eliminating veterinarian fees.

But it wasn't Pete Hines.

"Mornin', Coroner," drawled Sheriff Roy Blimline.

Doc Crowell touched his graying hair nervously.

"This *is* Doc Crowell, the County Coroner, ain't it?"

Doc Crowell scratched his beard stubble. He had been
appointed County Coroner two years ago because there had
been no one else available for the post. There had been

little demand on his talents as a public official. The inhabitants of the swamps and hills around Cypressville were
even less curious about how a man died, than why he had
been considered alive to begin with. Furthermore, Doc
Crowell was what is now whimsically referred to as an
"old-time country doctor." That is, he seemed to enjoy
administering to people, keeping them more or less alive
without puzzling himself as to why. He was happy bringing
life into the world, even though the results would often
have disturbed discriminating geneticists. Checking people
out, on the other hand, had never appealed to him.

He had forgotten momentarily that he was a coroner.
"Oh yes, sure, Sheriff," he said, finally, with forced levity.

"Looks like you're gonna earn tax-payer's money, Doc.
Seems we got ourselves a little old murder here."

"Murder?" Doc Crowell repeated vaguely.

"A humdinger too, Doc. Deceased been here quite a
spell." The Sheriff's laugh seemed to be half gravel. "Why,
I just can't hardly make hide nor hair of it!"

Doc Crowell was suddenly conscious of the pressing
mugginess of the hot, still morning. "Sorry to hear that,"
he said softly.

"Well, I ain't exactly. No missing person from around
here, and I figure it's a foreigner. Here's our chance to
solve us a murder, Doc! I ain't never had a chance to solve
me a real murder. Course there was Rabbit Martin getting
his head blowed off last summer, but everybody knowed
old man Allardice did it. No mystery there. I figure to sink
my teeth into one of them real murder mysteries."

"This town can always use some excitement," Doc Crowell said.

"I'll need your help, Doc. Big-city police always got one
of them medical examiners on the scene that later works
with the coroner. But you'll have to do double duty."

Doc Crowell hesitated. *It's her, he thought dully. It
couldn't be anyone else. He had managed not to think
about her much. But when he couldn't help himself, he
bought a bottle of I. W. Harper and that helped consid-*

erably. But maybe he had always known she would have to turn up sometime.

"Where did you find the body?" he asked, surprised at the calmness of his voice.

"Rabe's hounddog sniffed it out early this morning when Rabe was crossing Jones Culvert with a string of quail."

"Yes," Doc Crowell said as if to someone in the room. "Jones Culvert."

"I'm calling from the diner down the road a piece. You'll see mine and Rabe's car right off the road by the culvert when you drive out."

Doc Crowell sat for fifteen minutes unmoving in the parlor. It was an old parlor with a somewhat musty smell and nothing had been altered in it for at least ten years. The rising sun filtered in through the limp blinds by the tasseled lampshade and cast his thin, unsubstantial shadow on the flowered wallpaper. Finally, he stood up stiffly, feeling older than his fifty-three years, about as old, he thought as he went into the bathroom, as I'll be likely to get.

He doused his face with cold water and then glanced with only slight interest at the all-too familiar tired and genial face in the mirror.

As he tiptoed past the bedroom he saw, protruding from beneath a sheet, one of his wife's doughy legs, somehow resembling a detached limb from a waxworks. And there was a blessedly brief glimpse of her face, twisted even in sleep with self-pity and solidified futility.

He shook his head sadly as he walked toward his car. He felt sorry for Genevieve. He always felt guilty in some way for whatever had happened to her years ago. She had slowly turned to fat and constantly complained in a high crooning way. He hadn't even seen her body for years. The two of them had shared a mausoleum for the living. Or would one say, the walking dead?

But as he drove toward the town square, he mused in a desolate sort of way that it was Genevieve he should have

killed. If he had to kill anyone, it should have been Genevieve. Years ago. He would have been free. His life would
have been entirely different. He would have lived in another
town and perhaps done research. He had always wanted to
do medical research. Maybe he would have found a cure
for cancer by now. But Cypressville was Genevieve's home-
town, so here they had stayed. And here they had died, a
little at a time, destroying themselves with mutual, un-
analyzable spites and neglects and lacks of understanding.

Perhaps if murder ever improves anything, Genevieve's
murder, say twenty years ago, would have been a boon all
around. She wouldn't have degenerated and he would have
been free. More importantly Laura—had that been her
name?—Laura would still be alive. If he had been free all
those years, he would never have met or been interested in
Laura's type. And she would be alive, and the world would
be different now.

But of course that was ridiculous, wasn't it? Everything
was just as it was, and nothing could ever be any different.

He drove around the square, passed the statue of a
mounted Confederate soldier with his saber still raised and
fixed in the midst of a charge. Time seemed to have stood
still in Cypressville. Only the people had changed. They got
older and died, and before that, did things they couldn't
help and wondered why life couldn't have been some other
way.

He stopped outside of town, got a fresh bottle of I. W.
Harper from beneath the rear seat and took several long
pulls. He felt better by the time he reached the scene of
the crime. What had happened had simply been an inevitable necessity. He'd had to do it. And in any case, it
was done and could hardly be undone. But exactly what
had been done and by whom and why need never see the
light of day.

Eager as he was to be a sleuth, Sheriff Roy Blimline was
hardly an expert at criminal investigation. And, Doc Crowell mused as he got out of the car, I'm the one and only

coroner. Coroners are vital in solving crimes. Without a decent coroner's report, even expert criminal investigators were often handicapped.

Doc Crowell figured that his only problem would be that of appearing to do his duty in performing an autopsy, without at the same time incriminating himself.

Sheriff Roy Blimline scratched the sweating back of his florid neck and swished his Stetson about at hungry mosquitoes. He grinned and spat tobacco juice at a row of ants. "There it is, Doc. I say *it*," he grinned, " 'cause I don't rightly know if it's a he or a she."

Doc Crowell took a deep, careful breath, and peered down behind the rotting log. He was surprised at how little affected he was by the sight of the remains. Perhaps it was because time and the ravages of nature had so utterly altered its appearance, almost blended it into deep dark loam, decaying autumnal browns of ancient leaves, and damp mold.

"How long you figure it's been here, Doc?"

"Many months. But anyone could say that."

"I ought to know, Doc. It's important, I mean the proximate time of death and all."

Doc Crowell studied his public assignment with increasing detachment. "I realize that, Roy. I'll do my best to help."

"Ought to be a way of telling about when it happened."

"An effective autopsy ought to be done as soon as possible after death, Roy. Even then the time isn't always easy to figure."

"Well now, why ain't it? They don't have no trouble in the books I read!"

"Many factors involved, Roy. The most reliable way is from body changes. Especially, say, the contents of the stomach and the upper small intestine. The amount of digestion and the like. That can give a fair estimate. But here—too much time's passed. Remains badly decomposed and—well—the vital organs are missing. A very bad subject for a decent autopsy."

Roy poked with the toe of his boot. "No clothing, no jewelry. Nothing around like that. I figure the head and hands was cut off to avoid identification. That's why I figured right off it had to be homicide."

Doc Crowell wiped his forehead again.

"Well, you can tell if it's a man or woman, can't you, Doc?"

Crowell hesitated. He couldn't appear too dense, for he was generally known as a competent and fairly intelligent doctor. "The shape of the pelvis suggests a woman," he finally said, carefully. "But that's not conclusive proof. Many male and female skeletons are similar. You can be sure from an internal examination, but not in this case. Because of the missing vital organs."

Roy nodded gloomily. "Rats, wolves, worms, even birds, been at it for months."

Rabe's hounddog bayed hungrily from near the swamp. "Achin' to dig up the rest of the remains," Roy said.

"Might be difficult to prove it was murder," Doc Crowell said.

"Huh! With the head and hands cut off thataway?"

"Speculation isn't evidence, Roy. It isn't even possible now to tell if the mutilation occurred before or after death," Doc Crowell said truthfully. "Aside from the missing head, of course. The condition of the decomposed skin flaps here on the neck indicate they were cut, but it won't be easy, after this long a time, to tell when and how. Not even after a microscopic examination, but a complete autopsy might turn up something else."

"Well now it sure'n hoot had better turn up something!"

"Time's against us, Roy. After this long, what can we look for as the cause of death? Organs that might contain poison are missing. Was the victim hanged, bludgeoned, shot, knifed? After this long, you might find a bullet hole, or a bullet lodged somewhere in the remains. Might find what's left of a knife wound. Right now I don't see any such thing. Logical place to look for bullet holes or bludgeon marks is the skull. Isn't any skull. The victim might have been hanged, throttled, smothered, drowned, and there wouldn't be any way to tell that now."

Roy glumly spat tobacco juice. "We gotta know something."

"It would help considerably if you found the head, Roy. Help establish cause. Heads also help in positive identification because of the teeth. But then, the head may not be around here. It might be in another state."

"How you figure?"

"Can't tell when or how it happened now, Roy. Body that's had its position changed awhile after death, it shows flattening and some paleness in parts other than those in contact with the surface upon which it was in contact when discovered. You can tell by appropriate flatness of various body parts where a body's lain during periods of what's called primary flaccidity. But after this long, hard to say. Might have died months before it was put here. Can't say how, or when. At least not at this point."

"Now, Doc," Roy almost whined, "you make it sound like we don't stand a snowball's chance in hell solving this here homicidal mystery!"

"I'll do my best, Roy. What else can I say?"

"How can I figure motive without even knowing who the victim was? Not even knowing if it's male or female, or *nothin'*."

Roy pried the remains over with his boot, knelt down with a thick wheezing sigh and poked about with a stick in the dead pale area outlined by the shifted corpse. Small white bugs scurried out of the light. "Well now, why didn't I think of this before, Doc? It was put on these old leaves. They're from about the last growing season. So it was put here then!"

"Yes," Doc Crowell said in a peculiar whisper. "The last autumn."

Doc Crowell had the remains deposited on an old operating table in the storage room back of his office. He broke another bottle of I. W. Harper out from a store of a dozen bottles hidden in the filing cabinet. He took several long pulls, then donned rubber gloves and went to work. The whiskey helped preserve a somewhat abstract, philosophical attitude about the entire ambiguous situation. He was interrupted by several patients, including little Jamie Wheelis, who'd been bitten by a bumblebee which his stubborn mother kept insisting must have been a water moccasin. Old Man Jacobson came in with his back unhinged again and had to have it shot full of morphine and taped up before he could hobble home. Doc Crowell managed to complete a reasonable facsimile of an autopsy by 11:30.

It would be definitely unwise to put out a report that might appear too negligent. The State Attorney's office had started sending out spies to investigate backwoods autopsies. He took several swigs from his bottle, shoved it into a desk drawer in time to greet Roy Blimline.

Doc Crowell handed the anxious-faced sheriff a two-page report written in meticulous, slightly old-fashioned script.

X rays showed no bullets. Doc Crowell had found no bullets. He could find no indication of cause of death. There was still no proof of murder. Close approximation of height determined from length of main bones in each leg—right tibia, 363 mm long. Left tibia, 365 mm. According to the table, this put the height of victim in range of five feet four inches to five five and one-half inches. Deceased probably young, this having been determined by the front chest cartilages, especially those of the first ribs. Perhaps twenty years, or younger. Closer approximation of age could be determined by sending X rays to a competent anthropologist who could tell more from the spine, forearm and leg bones.

Remains of skin flap of severed neck tissue seemed to be cut. Same was true with tissue of wrists. All internal organs missing. Cut tissue examined by microscope, as well as could be done considering advanced decomposition, indicated no cellular reaction.

"What's that mean now, Doc?"

"That the cuts that severed hands and head were done postmortem."

Roy grinned bleakly. "Well now, that helps a whole hell of a lot, don't it? I sort of figured the deceased might have been running around without no head."

Doc Crowell smiled with strained tolerance. "You can always call yourself in another coroner, Roy. A real big-time forensic clinical pathologist from Palm City."

"Don't get up on your hind legs, Doc. I just got to have clues!"

"Then phone the State Attorney's office for help."

"You know I wouldn't go to those boys. Ah, Doc, we'll break this case, I know it!"

"Your faith moves me deeply," Doc Crowell said wryly.

He sat down behind his cluttered desk. His report was, so far, an honest one. Even without prejudice, it wouldn't be more complete, considering the limited facilities at his disposal. There was a dearth of evidence to be obtained here by autopsy. If any negligent backwoods autopsy report was exposed, however, there would be a scandal. They were cracking down. It would be difficult to say, Doc Crowell knew, how many murders escaped detection every year in isolated areas because of careless, incompetent, negligent and perhaps prejudicial autopsies. He wanted this one to bear up under outside scrutiny.

Suddenly Rabe Halloway and his triumphantly grinning hound burst in, spraying swamp mud on the walls. A Buster Brown shoebox was placed on the desk.

Looking into the box, Roy and Doc Crowell saw the hand.

Doc Crowell gazed at it wordlessly, while something like ice formed in his stomach. The hand was withered, brown. For a moment, it suggested a sort of insect, or perhaps a crab, imprisoned in the box.

"Go to work on it, Doc," Roy said gleefully. Then he, Rabe and the leering dog bounded across the street to Martha's Roost for beers.

Doc Crowell backed away from the box and stumbled against the filing cabinet. After hastily uncorking a fresh fifth of I. W. Harper and taking a few quick nips, he carried the box into the autopsy room. He managed, finally, to lift the hand out and put it on the table; then he sat heavily on a creaky chair in the dim, dusty light. There was no sound from outside in the hot muggy afternoon. A mud-dauber wasp buzzed somewhere up in the roof.

Doc Crowell blinked and wiped his face. The remains had an autumnal look and there was an oddly clean odor of dead leaves and damp loam. From the opposite corner, an old dusty osteology of human bones dangled from a rusty spring hook. Its polished skull jiggled subtly and its frozen grin seemed directed at Doc Crowell.

He remembered the other hand, the two hands together, raking with sharp fingernails at his face. He had been surprised at their resistant strength. They had been young hands. They had been strong with the will to live. They had surely surprised even themselves, the way they had tried to stay alive.

The eagerness of youth, he thought, and nipped quickly at the bottle. The blind, eager optimism of young reaching hands. Autumn is far away then. The seasons seem endless. But there comes a time when this yearning isn't quite so desperate a thing—

Why, Laura? Why did you turn a merely disagreeable mistake into an unending nightmare?

His eyes closed. He was oblivious to the sweat running down his face and dripping onto the front of his slightly soiled shirt. Sometimes when you're not so young, you also get desperate. You get desperate for the living you have never known.

Once, just once, after all these empty years, he had strayed—that was the often-used euphemism—strayed, strayed from the so very straight and narrow and dead. He had to admit that, with a wife like Genevieve, he had often been tempted. Then, during that sick call near Lockridge almost a hundred miles from Cypressville, there was Laura, the waitress, working late one night in a diner.

It didn't matter what her particular appearance or personality was. He couldn't really remember. It was just his time to stray. Later, too late, he recalled a predatory hunger in her eyes. He saw her a few times. There had been those stupid, naive, revealing little notes, the blunderings and fumblings and stupid, undignified mumblings of a wholly incompetent and tired roué.

Then that night he had driven her across the state line, back toward Cypressville. The threats began. The Mann Act, kidnaping, assault accusations. She had proven incredibly well-versed in sordid breaches of the law. She had those notes from him as evidence, and the ring he had bought her. Blackmail.

Thinking of the ring, he gave a dry lugubrious laugh and opened the middle desk drawer and looked at the box containing the ring. She had laughed when he asked her to give it back. But he had gotten it back just the same. Since then he hadn't looked at it.

He opened the box now and looked at the way the ring glittered in the wavering light. Then he shut the box with a snap and pushed it to the rear of the drawer, just as Roy came in.

"So what do you make out of that hand, Doc?"

"I'm afraid it's too decomposed for fingerprints."

"But what about that little ole missing finger?"

Doc Crowell leaned his forehead on his hand a moment. "What about it?"

Roy sighed. "Was it part of the mutilation?"

"Yes, the finger was removed postmortem."

"Robbery. The murderer got hasty about getting the ring off!"

"Maybe," Doc Crowell said, almost inaudibly.

"That was silver fingernail polish wasn't it, Doc?"

Doc Crowell looked up quickly. "Oh yes, the epithelial cells of the fingernails, they're very durable. They don't decay readily. Nor apparently does silver nail polish."

"So I figure the evidence adds up to the victim likely being a poor little ole girl," Roy said.

"It does seem likely now, doesn't it?"

"Silver nail polish ties in with what you said about the female pelvis, and the height and all. Now I got a little to go on, Doc! I got me a little ole girl, 'bout twenty or younger. Five feet four to five five and a half inches tall. Wore silver nail polish. Disappeared just about last October."

"I'm afraid that could include a great many girls, Roy."

"And, Doc, I'm awful sure the murderer is a local boy!"

Doc Crowell's heart was pounding inordinately loud. Illogically, he wondered if Roy might hear it thundering away in there like some piece of overworked machinery. "How do you figure that?"

"Because of where the body was hid, Doc. Somebody driving along U.S. 3, they knowed where to stop, so's to carry the body across the marsh without drowning himself in quicksand. They knew where to put that body so's there'd be a mighty poor chance of its being found for a long spell, if ever. Nobody who didn't know just where to walk would ever try crossing by the culvert. Somebody local had to know that."

"That's commendable reasoning," Doc Crowell admitted. Why, he thought, considering what he had already done, hadn't he been able to accept the added but practical outrage of tossing the body to the devouring quicksand?

Roy gave his gravelly laugh and slapped his thigh. "We're gonna wrap this ole murder up neat and quick, Doc! I've sent out info on this girl to all the towns around here. Figure the police might stir something out of a missing persons file."

Doc Crowell nodded heavily. "Don't forget me, Mr. Sherlock Holmes, if you dig up anything new."

Late afternoon, Rabe brought in the paper bag containing the right hand. It did not, Doc Crowell hastily volunteered, add further enlightenment to the crime. Roy sat, wiped his forehead, and stared at his muddy boots. "Got a call from Lockridge 'bout an hour back, Doc. Sheriff there name of Gregson. He thinks maybe this could be a girl, waitress, who has been missing there for nearly a year. Height, age, silver nail polish, all checks out. He's going on the assumption it could be the same girl. He's already started investigating among her friends and like that."

"Seems to me he's assuming a lot," Doc Crowell said.

Then Rabe ran in carrying a muddy Schlitz beer carton and yelping, much like his dog, that he had found the head.

The hound leaped over and thrust its dripping muddy muzzle into Doc Crowell's lap. He stared down into its smirking face with uncontrollable disgust.

Roy jumped up to call Gregson again in Lockridge. "Find out," he said, "what you can about that little ole head, Doc!"

When he was finally able to carry the head into the autopsy room, he stood hardly breathing in the stifling closeness. He nipped nervously at his bottle while the skeleton giggled silently on its rusty hinge spring. He hugged the bottle to his chest and sat thinking about the rather clinical subject of catabolism—the breakdown of dead tissue.

If Laura had been left in the swamp, she would soon have turned completely back into rich loam. No one—if she hadn't been discovered—would ever have known the difference. Alterations in a dead body are quite different from the natural cellular changes that occur in a live one. Life changes result in function, growth. Death, however, is considered a fast progression into nonfunction, wherein the cellular unit is broken down to the most basic elements. Function is destroyed. Death is destruction. The body in death is finally and forever consumed.

But was there really any basic difference?

Laura, there really isn't so much difference; so don't feel mad or disappointed or sad about it all. If there's a difference, it's only a matter of degree. Sometimes the living are really dead, but some of them don't seem to know it.

Doc Crowell stood up and belched.

At nine P.M. Roy enthusiastically inquired about the head, and was handed another page of the autopsy report. Marked postmortem decomposition. A considerable loss of soft tissue, making identification by facial appearance impossible. Some skin remained on the left side of the head and neck, apparently because it had been lying with that side down. The lowermost edge of the neck flap of the skin seemed to have been cut. Hair, probably blonde, hanging on the scalp tissue present on the left side. Skull or head indicated no cause of death. Skull intact, with no bullet holes.

Roy called Sheriff Gregson in Lockridge to pass on the added information, then turned to Doc Crowell beaming. "Missing waitress was a blonde!"

A few minutes later, a dentist sent over by Gregson from Lockridge rushed into the office. He soon finished examining the teeth of the deceased, after having fitted loose ones in their proper sockets. He then compared them with several dental X-ray plates he took from his briefcase. "Same girl," he said, then rushed out again.

Roy grabbed up the phone and told the good news to Gregson in Lockridge. He listened attentively after that, then hung up, sat down, and smugly tore off a chew of twist tobacco.

"She was just seventeen, Doc, but old in experience, according to Gregson. No parents. Lived with an alky uncle. Went out with near anything, so long as it wore pants with money in the pockets."

She looked much older, Doc Crowell thought. *Believe me, she looked a lot older than that. She said she was older, too, until we crossed the state line.*

Doc Crowell realized that his hands were unsteady and that they were also rather clammy.

"And they've got the murderer, too," Roy said.

A thrill of something close to terror worked unseen in

Doc Crowell as he sat up very straight. He looked at Roy
with exaggerated concentration, while something in his
stomach seemed to turn completely over. "A suspect?"

"Gregson's been working on him over there all afternoon."

"Is that so? And who is the murderer?"

"Kid name of Hal Bronson. Picked him up again on
suspicion. But he was a suspect all along, only Gregson
had no proof of what had happened to the girl. But now he
knows it was Laura Grendstedt. They been grilling that boy
something fierce! Man, they really been putting the screws
to that little ole boy!"

"Then he hasn't confessed?"

"He'll crack any minute, Gregson says. He sounds like a
real tough nut, this Sheriff Gregson does."

"And he's positive of *this* boy's guilt is he?"

As Roy talked, he occasionally went to the door and spat
into the darkness. Hal Bronson said that on the night Laura
disappeared, he had made a date to meet her at an old gas
station outside of Lockridge. His father was wealthy, and
he didn't want his old man to know the type of female
company he kept, so they met more or less in secret, or
tried to. Actually, the boy had been in trouble ever since
he'd been old enough to know the difference and only his
father's money had kept him from a few stretches in reform
school. He waited at the filling station for her. She
appeared, but with some other escort in a mud-splattered
car, the boy said. She laughed out the window at Bronson,
and the car drove on, heading down U.S. 3 in the direction
of Cypressville. Bronson insisted that that was the last he
ever saw or heard of Laura Grendstedt. But he couldn't
remember any license number, or the type of car. No one
else saw the car, but there were many witnesses who had
seen Bronson and the girl out together before. Unless the
mysterious "other escort" turned up, Gregson couldn't over-
look Bronson's admission that he was the last to see the
girl alive, and that he had made a date with her the night
she was killed.

"And what about this, Doc! He used to spend summers with his aunt, and his aunt was old lady Thorndike's sister who used to live out on U.S. 3, near the culvert where the body was found! So Bronson would know how to carry her across the swamp there without getting himself buried alive! Come to think of it, wonder why he wouldn't have just tossed her in that there quicksand."

After awhile, Doc Crowell looked up.

"So that makes it an open and shut case?" he said carefully.

"Gregson says that boy'll crack wide open like a rotten egg, Doc! Anyway, he's guilty."

"Is that right?"

"If he don't confess, they got an open and shut case again' him anyhow. He's been strictly no good since he was a pup! Now, Doc, we know that boy's *guilty!*"

Doc Crowell opened the middle desk drawer and took out a bottle of I. W. Harper and two glasses and put them on the desk. As he started to close the drawer, the ring box slid forward and looked up at him.

Roy's eyes bugged at the sight of the bottle. Everyone knew that Doc Crowell sometimes resorted to the bottle. But he also had a respected and dignified position in the community. In small towns like Cypressville, citizens are very understanding about other elderly, respected citizens who are forced by inexpressible vicissitudes of life to take refuge in a bottle now and then. More important, Doc Crowell was the only doctor available. And even more important was his congenial inability to dun patients for accumulated debts. Cypressville inhabitants were not only impoverished; they were noted for extreme frugality. Once, when Doc Crowell had ventured to up his house calls from two to three dollars, the general reaction suggested that he had been possessed by the devil and had sprouted horns. Everyone knew that if Doc Crowell collected half of what was owed him, he could have retired long ago to a life of idle luxury. So any self-righteous feelings regarding Doc Crowell's growing tendency to indulge in white lightning was held in abeyance. Nor could most citizens blame him, considering the kind of wife he was stuck with, for taking a drink now and then.

Still, Roy realized that it was going too far to flaunt his wickedness openly in this manner. Not that Roy minded a man's taking a drink. But the door was open. People were walking past. He stared at the bottle, then at Doc Crowell's gray, bearded face and the abnormal brightness of his eyes.

"Mouth's dry, Roy. Dry as onion skin," Doc Crowell said. He looked out at the night that was no longer clear. It was clouding over. The stars were disappearing like droves of frightened chickens, and a wind full of dampness was rising from the west.

He turned back toward Roy, poured the two glasses a third full of I. W. Harper, but made no move to drink.

"Well, Roy," he said, "you and Gregson happen to be idiots and A-number-one liars."

"Huh?"

"If you two got your only exercise jumping to conclusions, you'd be in great shape. You certainly would. I happen to know that Bronson is no more guilty than you are."

"Don't get your back up, Doc. Gregson ought to know. And anyway, how come you know so much?"

Doc Crowell held up his hand. "Because I'm guilty, Roy. That's how I know. That's how I know the Bronson boy isn't guilty. Scientifically, you might call it the law of excluded opposites, or—"

"Ah, *Doc!*" Roy looked at the bottle and shook his head.

"Yes, Roy, I killed Laura Grendstedt. With these skilled, practiced hands, I strangled that poor little girl. It seems unnecessary to point out that the murder method would hardly show up in an autopsy after so long a time."

Doc Crowell confessed everything, slowly, calmly, in the way he told tall and dryly humorous stories summer evenings over in the Square.

Roy listened, his head continuing to shake in a steady, rhythmical denial, like the head of one of those mechanical toys. His mouth hung open. A stream of tobacco juice unthreaded like black string from the corner of his mouth.

"Ah, Doc, you've sure been hitting that bottle hard, but why'd you want to joke about a thing like that?"

"She was trying to blackmail me, Roy. That's no joke. She was laboring under the naive opinion that a doctor must always be rich. But of course I couldn't pay. And she threatened to expose me. Everyone would have known. Such as it is, Roy, I appreciate the respect bestowed upon me by this community."

Roy gave an uneasy laugh and wiped his face. *"You, Doc?"*

"When I explained the facts, she laughed and refused to believe me. We were parked out there a mile north of the culvert. Other cars were approaching. She tore her dress. She threatened to jump out of the car and flag down one of those approaching cars and lie about how she arrived at her disheveled state, accuse me of atrocious acts. That was when I did it, Roy. But it wasn't quite so cold or calculated as that. It was like a dream—there was a lot of resentment and hate stored up in me, no doubt. I exploded. Before I realized what I was doing, I—it was done."

Roy managed another wavering laugh. "You couldn't do such a thing, Doc. That's the first time I ever heard you fail to put over a story."

"It seemed unlikely to me, too, until after it was done, Roy. We don't know one another. But we know ourselves even less, Roy; I'm convinced of it."

"I'll never buy that story, Doc!" He tossed off the whiskey, and with unsteady hands poured himself another double shot. "You can't sell me that."

"I'm afraid you'll have to accept it, Roy."

"Not me, Doc. Peddle that story anywhere, and who would believe it? Nobody would."

"She laughed at me. I was old and ridiculous. There were many reasons, but I did it. Maybe anyone could do it if the circumstances are right." His voice trailed away as he looked out the window. It had begun to rain.

"It's the people here, Roy. I thought of all the people around here who depend on me. I help them, Roy, keep them well and happier because I know them. I've brought them into this world, and I know them better than anybody else ever could. And I'd have gone to jail, and they wouldn't have had anyone around then who gave a tinker's damn whether they lived or died." He smiled. "The one patient I didn't know very well was myself."

"Nobody around these parts will believe that story, Doc."

"But I'm sorry I did it, Roy. No matter why. It can't be justified, can it? I'm sorry, because it hurts to be murdered. I know, Roy, because I've been hurting for years."

Doc Crowell stood up and looked into a mirror over the washbasin at his wavering reflection. "Who am I? Who are you, Roy? Tracking down murderers is a futile business isn't it, Roy? A murder case only begins when it's supposed to be over, when the murderer is caught and sufficiently punished. Because, unless you can find out why he really did it, Roy, you've never really solved anything. Have you?"

"We've solved this one, Doc. Gregson and me. And you helped. The kid's over there in Lockridge and he'll crack any minute and confess."

"No, Roy. I'm the murderer. Genial, kind old Doc Crowell." He chuckled. "Laura died rather suddenly and young. It's taken me considerably longer, that's the only difference. Listen, Roy, you've got to be careful about jumping to quick conclusions about anything—especially about decomposing bodies." He tapped himself on the chest. "In the instance of this body, for example. An attempt to guess at the cause of death here would undoubtedly be foolish and a waste of time."

Roy's grin was more confident as he stood up and reached for the bottle. "Guess I might as well get plastered along with you, Doc. You must be getting sort of lonely away over there by yourself." He poured both glasses half full, lifted his and grinned more broadly at Doc Crowell. "You sure must have been hittin' this old stump water good and hard, Doc. I never heard nobody talk so wild and crazy since old Allardice got hisself hanged."

"I see you're going to be stubborn about this."

"You're loaded plumb to the gills, Doc, that's all. Not even in your right mind. I know you too well. You're just crazy enough to want to save that kid's life. Ain't that it, Doc?"

Doc Crowell shook his head. "I should be flattered by your desire to turn me into a saint and a martyr, Roy, but I'm afraid I'm not. I'm confessing to this murder, and you've got to arrest me!"

"Sure, sure, Doc." Roy laughed and wiped his mouth. "Drunk as a coot. Figurin' to save that little ole kid's worthless hide. Why he's never been no good. That boy ought to have been drown in the rainbarrel before his eyes got opened, like a little ole pup's."

Doc Crowell jerked open the desk drawer and took out the ring box. "You have no proof at all against that boy. Only circumstantial evidence and maybe a forced confession. I have incontrovertible proof here, Roy. Proof, understand, absolute positive proof of my guilt!"

Roy looked at Doc Crowell and his eyes wavered to the ring box, then back to Doc Crowell's steady too bright gaze. At that moment, Rabe yelled from out in the street that Roy had a call from Gregson's office in Lockridge. And Roy said, "Just hold your horses 'til I come back, Doc."

Doc Crowell watched Roy go out the door, and after that he sat looking at the box on top of his desk. Once he walked to the door of the storage room and looked in. He returned to the desk, sat down and took a long bolstering pull from the bottle before Roy appeared in the doorway. There was an odd look on Roy's face, a strange mixture of sad triumph.

Roy came on in, turning his Stetson nervously in his hands.

"Too late now to help that kid anyway, Doc." He lifted

a glass of I. W. Harper from the table. "So let's drink to a successful murder case, wrapped up and put away!"

"What do you mean, too late?"

"Suicide, Doc. Guess that don't leave any doubt that crazy, no-good kid was guilty, does it?"

"Suicide?"

"That's right. Bronson just hanged himself in his cell half an hour ago."

Doc Crowell sat for some time, not saying anything, looking into the rainy dark and gripping the ring box in his right hand. Then the phone rang and reflexively he lifted the receiver. A tired smile stitched its way across his face. Finally, he said with mock impatience, "You just calm down, Pete Hines. Your old lady's not ready yet, you ought to know that. She's had enough experience by now she doesn't need me anyway. Just don't get anxious and I'll be out there before morning."

He put the ring box back into the desk drawer and closed it before he stood up and wearily reached for his hat.

ONE MAN'S FAMILY   Richard Hardwick

THE FARREL BROTHERS, Roger and Paul, were eleven and twelve years old respectively when their father sat down with them and told them the facts of life in a straight-from-the-shoulder manner. The facts of life, that is, as he, Horatio Farrel, saw them. There was nothing in this paternal revelation that touched on matters biological, no mention of birds or bees or salmon valiantly fighting their way upstream. That sort of thing was the work of nature, and as far as Horatio Farrel was concerned, nature could handle it. The facts he set out to clarify to his sons were the man-made facts, law, ethics, contractual obligations, interest, compound and simple, and the many ways of getting the upper hand and keeping it. He stressed the importance of position, of early goals, and the importance of letting absolutely nothing stand in your way in the unqualified pursuit of these goals.

In summation, Horatio Farrel hooked his thumbs in his vest and said, "These things, Roger and Paul, are the life blood, the mainstays, the very heart of existence in this day and time. Success and integrity, in that order, are the concepts to keep constantly before you. By these things a man is measured. Pick your target in life, set it high, and never let yourself be deterred!"

He stopped and looked down at his sons as if expecting applause.

"Like you, Dad?" said Roger, who was eleven, and had already skipped one grade successfully. "I mean you being president of the bank and on all those board of directors and things?"

"Boards of directors," he corrected. "And yes, that is precisely what I meant. I have driven myself to the uttermost in every endeavor I have undertaken throughout my life. I want you boys to do the same for the good name of Farrel!"

"I made all A's on my report card, Dad," Roger said.

"I know you did, son. And I am proud of you."

Roger turned toward his older brother, who was in the same grade at school. "What'd you make on your report card, Paul?" he said, with a sly grin.

Paul squirmed and avoided his father's eyes. "I tried, Dad. I did the best I possibly could. Honest."

The elder Farrel frowned darkly. "I was just about to bring this up, Paul. It appears that you are barely getting by. Now, there must be a reason for this."

"I'm just not as smart as Roger."

"Nonsense! If your brother can do it, then so can you! Next semester I want to see improvement, son, I want to see improvement!"

Paul hung his head and nodded. Roger stifled a giggle.

Paul Farrel did try harder. Yet the harder he tried, the more strenuous the effort he made, the farther he seemed to lag behind the accomplishment of his brother. And so they went through high school, Roger at the head of the class, riding the crest, and Paul bringing up a sorry rear.

Somehow, Paul managed to hang on, and he graduated at the same time Roger did, though there were those who thought it was done deliberately by the teachers, some of whom owed money to Horatio Farrel's bank, and some who simply wanted to get such a dumbhead out of the school.

The boys went on to the university, the alma mater of

their father, and their father's father before him. Roger, to the surprise of no one, became president of the freshman class. Paul, on the other hand, blended in with the hundreds of other freshmen, distinguishable only by the fact that he was Roger Farrel's brother. Again, it was Roger who amazed the professors with his grades and leadership qualities, while Paul struggled along like a young bull mired in quicksand.

His father's displeasure was not hidden. "You simply are not making the effort your brother is!" said Horatio Farrel during the Christmas holidays. Then, in an unexpected amelioration of his tone, "I know how it is with a lad of your age, Paul, away at school for the first time, just beginning to feel his oats." The father gave a short lascivious chuckle. "By gad, I'm not so old that I can't remember the attraction of a well-turned coeducational ankle! However, time is not to be frittered away! Regardless of what you may hear elsewhere, the meek will most certainly *not* inherit the earth! It is the strong, son, the ones who drive on against all odds, who are deflected by absolutely *nothing* —those are the ones who make it!"

"I think I'm just dumb, Dad," said the dejected and chastised Paul. "They gave us some tests up there at school, some IQ tests and stuff like that, and I didn't do so good on them. Maybe I ought to go to something like a trade school—"

"Trade school!" Horatio Farrel exploded. "A son of *mine!* Bosh! And as for these tests, all that's so much non-sense! Pay no attention to it! You, sir, are a Farrel, which means you are the peer of any man! Now, you get to work."

Paul nodded. "Yes, Dad. But I don't think—"

Horatio Farrel, however, had picked up his *Wall Street Journal*. He snapped it open crisply, which always meant all conversation was over and done.

Quite naturally, the situation did not change because of the things Horatio Farrel had told his son. The remainder of the four college years were a repetition of the first.

Roger Farrel shone like a bright comet streaking over the campus, a young man destined for the top in whatever he chose to do, while Paul continued to grind away, a sluggish fish going against the rapids, calling on every cell in his brain in order to stay on with barely passing grades. And always behind him, pushing, cajoling, threatening, was Horatio Farrel.

At graduation, Roger Farrel took his degree *summa cum laude,* and gave the class valedictory address, which in itself was better than the average address. As he spoke confidently, a Phi Beta Kappa key dangled from his watch chain.

Had the diplomas been presented in order of standing rather than alphabetically, Paul Farrel would have been the last student to leave the ceremony.

A short holiday ensued, after which Roger and Paul were put to work in the family bank. They began as tellers, it being Horatio Farrel's intention to acquaint his sons with every phase of the operation before their installation as officers. Roger breezed through the simple chores, and well before the first year was out was sitting behind a desk, on which was a mahogany plaque inscribed in gold letters with his name, and the title *Asst. Cashier.* Six months more and the title behind Roger's name read, *Asst. Vice-President,* while Paul still remained behind his teller's bars, his head wreathed in unbalanced adding-machine tapes, his face a display of perplexity to the banking public.

"Are you trying, son?" Horatio Farrel inquired one afternoon as two bookkeepers labored over Paul's deposit slips and cashed checks. "Are you really pulling *with* us, boy?"

He could only reply as he had always done. "I'm doing the best I can, Dad. Maybe I'm not cut out for this kind of work. Maybe—"

"Well, what in heaven's name kind of work *are* you cut out for!" Horatio Farrel bellowed, jowls quivering and face growing red.

"I always did have trouble with figures," mused Paul,

watching in admiration as one of the bookkeepers danced his fingers over the keys of the adding machine. "Maybe I ought to go to a trade school—"

Paul was transferred from pillar to post, throughout the bank. The mess he made in bookkeeping was truly monumental. His second day as a runner, Paul lost an envelope containing over twenty-one thousand dollars in bank clearings. Fortunately, a little old lady recovered the envelope and returned it to the bank, but it did make the point clear and final to Paul Farrel. The morning following this incident a note was found pinned to Paul's bed. It was addressed to his father, and at breakfast, the elder Farrel read it.

Dear Dad, [it began]
  I have caused more than my share of trouble for you and the bank. I have left town to make my fortune on my own. I have also borrowed fifty dollars from your wallet—

Horatio Ferrel dropped the letter to the table and quickly drew out his billfold. A quick thumbing revealed a sixty-dollar shortage.

"Can't even *count!*" he muttered, and picked up the letter again.

—and I will pay you back with interest at six percent as soon as I can. (If I can figure the interest, ha, ha!) I will let you know when I am a success.

                                   Your son,
                                   Paul (Farrel)

"I say it's good riddance, Dad," Roger said, helping himself to a second stack of wheatcakes.

Horatio Farrel crumpled the letter and tossed it aside. "I suppose you're right, Roger. Perhaps we are better off without Paul." He reached across the table and picked up his *Wall Street Journal*, snapped it open, and began to stir his coffee as he read.

Exactly one year later an envelope arrived in Horatio Farrel's morning mail. In the envelope was a money order in the amount of fifty-three dollars, and a letter. The postmark was that of a lakeside city in the midwest.

Horatio Farrel looked at the money order. The name of the sender was Paul Farrel. "Must have gotten somebody to figure the interest for him!"

Then he read the letter:

Dear Dad,

A lot of things have happened to me since I last saw you. I am working my way through a trade school here, and I am doing well even if I do say so myself. I have not forgotten all· the things you told me. Here is the money I took.

Your son,
Paul (Farrel)

"Trade school, indeed!" Horatio Farrel groused. He stuck the money order into his pocket, tossed the letter in the wastebasket, and opened the *Wall Street Journal*.

After that, with the exception of a cheap card each Christmas, nothing was heard of Paul Farrel for nearly fifteen years. And then one morning an inconspicuous black sedan drove into the city. It was a Saturday morning, and the car, with its lone occupant, drove directly to the bank. The driver unlocked the front door of the bank with a key and stepped inside, closing the door behind him and locking it.

He walked with a brisk step across the empty lobby, past the teller cages, and paused before a door.

Behind the door Horatio Farrel, white-haired, bent, yet still with a sharp gleam in his eye and with no intention of throwing over the traces, sat at his desk, alone in the vast marble temple erected by his own father. As he pored over the papers before him, there came a knock at the door.

"Yes! Yes! Who is it!" the old man said testily.

The huge door opened a crack and a face peered in. "Dad?"

The old man squinted, then lowered his head and peered through his bifocals. "Eh? Who's that? Roger?"

"It's me, Dad. It's Paul."

The door swung open and a tall straight man entered the office. He was clad in a business suit that was both expensive and conservative.

"Paul?" said the old man. "Paul?" He pushed the papers aside and came to his feet.

Paul Farrel strode across the deep carpet with catlike self-assurance, a trait Horatio Farrel did not remember in his older son. Gone was the diffidence, the hang-dog look, and in their stead was a quiet exudation of confidence. Here without a doubt, was a man who knew what he was doing and where he was going.

"It *is* you, boy! Why it's been—it's been . . . "

"Sixteen years, Dad. Almost to the day."

"Sit down, son! Sit down! How about a cigar?" The old man slid a teakwood humidor across the desk. Paul dipped his fingers in, took out a cigar and sniffed it. He nodded his head in approval.

The old man resumed his seat. "Now! Tell me about yourself! I see you've done well, Paul. No doubt you gave up that stupid trade-school idea."

"Not exactly, Dad."

"Will you be in town long? Yes sir, I want to hear all about you!"

"Just here today," said Paul, lighting the cigar and blowing a cloud of blue smoke toward the distant ceiling.

"Business?"

Paul Farrel nodded. "Business."

"Well now, that is a shame! What about you, boy? You know, you never let Roger or myself know a thing, just those cards at Christmas. Are you in some kind of hush-hush thing, son? Secret work?"

"You might say that, Dad. I made it to the top, just the way you always wanted Roger and me to do. It was tough.

There were times when I felt unsure of myself, felt that I couldn't go through with it. But whenever I felt that way, I remembered the things you drummed into me, Dad. Never let anything stand in your way, you said. Drive a hard bargain, and always stick to it once it's made."

"Wonderful! Wonderful!" cackled the old man. "Now this business you have in town, who is it? What's it about?"

"It's with you," Paul said, pointing off-handedly at his father with the end of his cigar.

"Business with *me?* What could it be?"

"This," Paul said. He put his cigar in the ashtray with a steady hand and reached inside his tailored jacket. The hand came out holding a snub-nosed revolver.

Horatio Farrel stared at the gun, and slowly he began to rise to his feet behind the desk.

"I believe it would be better if you remained seated, Dad. And don't worry, it won't hurt. I never believed in hurting people." He gave a little chuckle. "Haven't had a complaint yet."

"What—what are you going to do with *that* . . . " Horatio Farrel said, his eyes glued to the gun. "Some kind of joke . . . is that it . . . ?"

"Afraid not, Dad. Now if you'll sit down—"

"You—you can't—"

"I have to. This is my business, my trade."

"But I'm—I'm your *father!* You *can't* . . . "

"It's nothing personal, Dad. It's a simple contract, no more, no less. You know I couldn't back out on a contract. Why, my reputation would be ruined. Now, if you'll just hold still."

"Paul . . . Paul, there must be some mistake . . . " The old man pushed his chair back from the desk and leaped with surprising agility. He dashed around the far side of the desk and broke for a second door, on which was lettered, *Roger Farrel, Executive Vice-President.* He reached the door, found it locked, and began to pound on it with his fists.

"*Roger!*" he screamed. "*Roger Help! HELP!*"

Paul Farrel padded across the room behind him. He shook his head, and as if explaining something to a child, he said, "Roger's not in there. Nobody's here but you and me. It was Roger who hired our firm." He looked at the gold-leafed title behind his brother's name. "Roger wants to be president of the bank, Dad."

Paul Farrel lifted the revolver, and very professionally squeezed the trigger.

YOU CAN TRUST ME Jack Ritchie

MIKE NEELAND wouldn't pay the two hundred thousand dollars, so he was getting Sam Gordon back—piece by piece.

The little finger lay on cotton in a small cardboard box open on the desk. "That came yesterday," Neeland said. "I can expect a little more in today's mail." He glanced at his watch. "And that would be at one-thirty."

I studied the finger for a few seconds and then sat down. It was something new for me to act like a detective—about as different as you could get. I usually put people away for Neeland, not find them. "Why don't you pay?" I asked.

Mike puffed his panetella. "What's Gordon to me anyway? Just a bum in a tuxedo. I pay him one-fifty a week to help keep things under control at the Blue Moraine. I don't even remember the color of his eyes."

"Brown," his wife Eve Neeland said. She smiled faintly and lazily. "I notice everybody's eyes."

The wrapping the box had come in told me that it had been mailed in North Lancaster, just across the state line, at ten-thirty the night before. "Why should anybody figure that you'd part with two hundred thousand to get Gordon back?"

Neeland shrugged. "Maybe Gordon talked bigger than he

was and somebody believed he was like a brother to me, or
my right arm."

I read the block-penciled note:

WE'VE GOT MORE OF GORDON AND PROMISE
REGULAR DELIVERY. WHEN YOU'RE READY
TO PART WITH THE TWO HUNDRED THOU-
SAND, PUT AN AD IN THE LOST AND FOUND
COLUMN OF THE JOURNAL. LOST. BLACK
AND WHITE TERRIER. ANSWERS TO NAME
OF WILLI. WE'LL GET IN TOUCH WITH YOU.

I wasn't serious when I asked the next question. "Why
not go to the police?"

Neeland laughed. "Danny, if this was something simple,
like just murder, I might for kicks let the cops here handle
it. I pay some taxes like anybody else and besides a few of
the precinct captains earn more from me than from the
city. But kidnaping is federal stuff. I couldn't keep the work
local. And once the federal boys get one foot inside anybody's door, they got the habit of looking in four directions.
I spent twenty years building this organization and I'm not
going to have it fall on my ears because of a punk like
Gordon. I'm not anxious to have the F.B.I. signing me up
for a TV quiz before Congress."

And that was the answer, of course. That's why some
people expected Neeland to part with the money. To keep
the troubles in the family.

Eve caressed a wave of honey hair back into place. "In
that case why not pay what they want? I don't think two
hundred thousand is going to break you, or even make a
little bend."

"It's still a lot of money and I don't want to start a habit.
Other ambitious people might get the idea that it's a new
indoor sport to get money out of me if I let this thing pass."
Neeland scowled. "I just want to know one way or the other
who's got the crazy nerve to try to pull something like this

on me. And when you find that out, Danny, you can get rid of them any way you like. Any way at all."

Eve tamped a cigarette on the shiny desk. "Why not bail Gordon out first and then go out after whoever has him?"

I smiled. "Gordon's still got nine fingers and ten toes. And there's still more than those digits to work on. So we've got time. If Mike pays now, the people who have Gordon will find the whole world to hide in. But if he keeps things the way they are, they've got to stick around this part of the country."

Eve's gray eyes turned to me. "You're sure cold-blooded," she said. But it sounded like a compliment.

Neeland laughed. "Danny never loses sleep after any job I give him."

"You got an organization right here," I said. "When you're not using me, I suppose you put some of your help to work?"

"Sure. But they're punks. All of them. And that's my fault because that's the way I pick them. I don't like any-body too smart in the organization." He studied me. "I import you in, Danny, for the more delicate jobs because you got the brains not to make mistakes and embarrass me. But I wouldn't want you around all the time. I'd get nervous about it."

"How long has Gordon been gone?"

"A week. I was supposed to put the two hundred thou-sand in a briefcase and see that it was dropped at the inter-section of J and 41 ten miles out of town at eleven last Tuesday night. I tried being cute. Left a dummy package full of newspaper strips instead and had three of my boys staked out near the place. They picked up a weasel char-acter when he stopped his beat-up car and reached for the package. We took him to a place where nobody can hear screams and asked him questions. His name was Baini, but he was a nothing. He never heard of Gordon. That I'll swear to, because he was willing to tell us anything—his grandmother's maiden name if we were interested. All he knew was that he got a phone call and a promise of fifty bucks if he performed the errand. He was supposed to take the briefcase back to his room and wait until somebody called for it. He couldn't even give a description of whom to expect."

"I suppose you sent somebody to Baini's room to wait?"

Neeland nodded. "But nothing doing. There are a couple of hills at J and 41 and the moon was bright. They must have been watching and seen us pick up Baini. I got a note the next day. They said that if I tried anything like that again, they'd cut Gordon's throat."

"And so?"

Neeland grinned. "And so I let it ride. I was hoping they'd do that little thing and get the hell out of the country. But now I see they're still in business."

"Who knows Gordon is gone?"

"Just the three of us in this room and the three boys who picked up Baini. They're not too bright, but they know how to keep their mouths shut. I don't like to have the news spread around."

"Do they know that you're now getting part of Gordon?"

"No. Not that. They might get restless and think I'm not a good type boss to work for if I let that happen to one of my help." Neeland lit a fresh cigar. "Gordon worked at the Blue Moraine. That's one of my places at the county line. He's got a wife. Dorothy. But she doesn't know that anything's happened. Whoever's got Gordon didn't bother to let her know about—figuring she doesn't have the two hundred grand, I suppose. I told her that I sent Gordon off to San Francisco on a little errand. He'd be gone awhile."

"She believed that? He left without packing or saying good-bye?"

"I told her Gordon didn't have the time. It was a hurry-up job for me."

"What did Gordon look like?"

"Around six feet. Lot of white teeth. That's about it. Like I said, he was practically a stranger."

There was a knock at the door and an elderly shirt-sleeved porter came in. "Your mail, Mr. Neeland."

Neeland took the letters and the small package and nodded the porter out of the room.

Eve Neeland rose. "I've seen fingers before." She picked up her coat and left the room.

Neeland used a pen knife to cut away the string from the package. He unwrapped it and lifted the cover. "It's what I expected."

From the curve of the finger, I guessed that it had come from the right hand. The post mark on the wrapping indicated that it had been mailed the night before in Griffin, a river town twenty-five miles west. This time there was no note. They figured Neeland already had the message.

I put on my hat. "I might as well drive over to the Blue Moraine. It's as good a place as any to start."

Neeland nodded. "I'll phone ahead to see that you get cooperation."

I left him and went through the big room of the Parakeet. This was the club Neeland called his headquarters, but he had at least a half a dozen others in this county alone. The place was cleaned up for tonight's business, except for a technician who had one of the roulette wheels apart and was checking for dips.

The Blue Moraine was located in the rolling hills twenty miles outside of town. It had been built to look like a highway restaurant, but that fooled nobody—if anybody needed fooling.

The bar was big and cool and, except for the single bartender and a thin fair man on a stool, it was deserted.

The thin man spoke. "Regan?"

I nodded.

"Neeland phoned and told me to expect you. I'm Van Camp. I manage the place for Mike."

He ordered two bourbons. "What can I do for you?"

"I'd like to know about Sam Gordon. Whatever you can tell me."

He raised an eyebrow. "He's in trouble?"

"Maybe."

When I said nothing more, he shrugged. "Nothing much to tell. He hasn't been in here for a week. He's just another boy here. Looks good in a tuxedo. Just like one of the customers. Pretty big. Your size. A nondrinker. Never saw much of him outside of working hours. That's about all I know. I don't associate with the help."

The bartender brought the drinks and moved away.

"What's this all about?" Van Camp asked.

"Neeland didn't tell you?"

"No."

I sipped my drink. "Then you wouldn't want to know."

He shrugged again. "All right. I wouldn't want to know."

"When was the last time you saw Gordon?"

"A week ago."

"Where do you think Gordon is?"

"I wouldn't know. Maybe he's on a drunk."

"You said he didn't drink."

He was faintly irritated. "Not during working hours, he didn't. What he did away from the place I wouldn't have any idea."

"Who does?"

"I suppose his wife would know. Why don't you ask Dorothy?"

"How many other people do you have here? With jobs like Gordon's, I mean."

"Three. Joe, Fred, and Pete."

"What's the name of Joe's wife?"

"How would I know?"

"And Pete's wife?"

He saw what I was getting at. "Gordon brought Dorothy in one evening and introduced me."

"You've got a fine memory. Or was she that impressive?"

He glared at me. "Ask me about Gordon. Why don't you just stick to him?"

I glanced around the big barroom. "You do your real business upstairs? That's where the tables are?"

He nodded.

"Nice place."

His mouth got tight. "It should be. It's built the way I paid for it."

I smiled. "But now you just manage it? Neeland bought in?"

He picked up his drink. "You might say that."

"Does it leave a bitter taste?"

The bartender came over to me. "Mr. Neeland's on the line. He wants to talk to you, Mr. Regan."

I went to the wall phone behind one end of the bar and picked up the dangling receiver. "Regan."

Neeland was worried. "They sent a note to Gordon's wife."

"She called you?"

"That's right. She says she's going to the police if I don't get Gordon back right away."

"Can't you stall her a couple of days more?"

"A few hours was all I could manage. She knows that Gordon's coming back piece by piece now and she doesn't like the idea at all."

"You want me to talk to her now?"

"I guess so. I can't think of anything else. I told her you'd be over."

I tapped a cigarette out of my pack with one hand. "Suppose I can't do anything?"

He hesitated. "Then I guess I'll have to pay the two hundred thousand. I haven't got any choice." He gave me Dorothy Gordon's address and hung up.

She lived in one of the old, red-brick apartment buildings on the east side. When she opened her door I saw that she had big dark eyes, a small face, and was on the edge of being pretty.

Apparently she was one of those women who believe in tugging at a handkerchief in moments of stress. "Mr. Regan?"

"Yes. I've come to help you."

She shook her head. "Nobody can help me except Mr.

Neeland. He's simply got to pay the money they want."

"Why?"

Her eyes widened. "Why? Because—because they're cutting—"

"I mean, why should Neeland be the one to pay?"

"But he has the money, doesn't he?"

"That's what somebody figures. But why should Gordon be worth two hundred grand to him?"

She seemed horrified that I could think a thing like that. "Sam worked for him."

"They probably exchanged less than fifty words a year."

"But—but I'd pay the money, if I had it."

"He's your husband, but he's nobody to Neeland." There was a colored framed photograph on one of the side tables. Sam Gordon had wavy hair and a half-smile that was meant to be devastating. He was the type they cast as chariot riders in Cinemascope. You just knew he had pretty muscles.

Dorothy Gordon gave the handkerchief another tug. "If Mr. Neeland doesn't pay, I'm going right to the police."

"If the kidnapers find that out, they'll undoubtedly kill your husband."

Her hands moved helplessly. "But there's nothing else I can do. I can't let them—do what they're doing to Sam."

"How long you been married?"

She dabbed at her eyes. "Three years."

"And how long has he been working?"

"Just this last year. Ever since—" She stopped.

I finished for her. "Ever since your money was gone?"

She flushed. "That's none of your business."

I wondered how much money she had brought into the marriage. A man who knows himself to be as darling as Gordon's smirk showed usually doesn't marry for nothing.

"I'm going to call the police," she said with final determination.

"Give me a couple of hours."

"Why? You won't be able to get my husband back."

"I can try. Just a couple of hours. Until five."

She seemed undecided, as though she were looking for someone to make the decision for her.

"Look," I said. "If I don't come up with anything by five, you can call the police. Now let's see the note they sent you."

She went to a French desk against the wall and brought back the piece of paper.

The words were again in block printing:

MRS. GORDON. WE HAVE YOUR HUSBAND AND WE WANT TWO HUNDRED THOUSAND DOLLARS FOR HIM. THE MAN WHO CAN GIVE THAT IS MIKE NEELAND, BUT HE'S BEING STUBBORN. YOUR HUSBAND HAS LOST TWO FINGERS ALREADY AND CAN LOSE MORE. ASK NEELAND FOR THE DETAILS.

I handed the note back. "Tell me about your husband. How does he spend the day?"

"Well, he usually works at the Blue Moraine from nine at night until four or five in the morning, depending on how much the play at the tables has thinned out."

"And then?"

"He usually comes back home and sleeps until noon."

"Usually?"

"Always. Then he eats breakfast. And then . . . " She thought it over. "Then he'd go to a movie or the beach."

"Alone?"

"With me."

"And then?"

"We'd come home and—read until it was time for him to go to work."

"I'd like to have a snapshot of your husband."

She went back to the desk and came back with a black and white photograph. "But remember," she cautioned. "If I don't hear from you by five o'clock, I'm going to phone the police."

I drove back to the Parakeet.

Eve Neeland was in one of the booths in the barroom. "Ah," she said, "the man who walks like a detective."

I got a drink and brought it to her booth.

She looked over the rim of her glass. "How are you doing?"

"I'm moving. That's about all." I took out the snap of Gordon.

She glanced at it. "He likes himself, doesn't he?" She met my eyes and smiled slightly. "You're not pretty. I guess you're glad to hear that. I've been watching you."

"Don't you watch them all?"

"You mean did I watch Gordon?"

"You're the one who said it."

"Well, he never made it, Danny boy. He was a peasant with ideas. About me and more. But I don't get used as a stepladder."

"Of course Mike doesn't know a thing about it?"

"Now that was a silly question."

"You get bored pretty easy, don't you?"

"With some people. Now you might be something different."

"Does Mike interest you?"

"Almost. But the days are long." The gray eyes were speculative. "Mike is a worker. He gets there by making everything a steady job. It took him twenty years to build what he has. How long would it take you?"

"It's not my line of work."

She smiled. "Has any woman ever held on to you for long?"

"Where's Mike?"

"In his office."

I finished my drink and got up.

She watched me. "You'll be back. Sometime."

Mike Neeland was going over the books with one of his accountants. He shooed the man out of the office. "How's it going?"

"I may be on to something. Dorothy Gordon's giving me until five to do something spectacular. Do you know where this Baini lives?"

"Sure, but I think you're heading into a dead end. He doesn't know a thing." Neeland searched his memory. "He's got a room on the east side on Jackson. A run-down hotel called the Sterling."

At the Sterling, the desk clerk knew the answer without having to look it up. "Baini's in 407."

"Is he in?"

"More than likely. He can't get around too much right now." The clerk looked me over. "Accident, I guess. I'm not nosey. I told him to go to the hospital, but he won't."

The musty self-service elevator took me to the fourth floor. I softly tried the doorknob of 407, but the door was locked. I knocked.

The voice was muffled. "That you, Al?"

If that was the key to get in, I'd use it. "Yeah."

I waited half a minute before I heard the key turn. Baini's eyes widened when he saw I wasn't Al and he tried to close the door again.

I pushed my way in, using a hand on his chest. The shove wasn't hard, but he cried out and toppled over. I saw why when I closed the door. Both his feet were bound with bandages, strictly a do-it-yourself job. He lay on the floor moaning until he finally decided to crawl to the brass-frame bed. He sank down on the edge of it, his mind still on the pain.

Baini was a small man in his twenties with black darting eyes that saw a lot but never learned anything. His face was swollen and the color varied from putty to purple. Mike's boys must have started there before they tried being more subtle.

When he managed to look at me, I said, "Who's Al?"

He licked his lips. "A porter here. He brings me my meals."

"Did you tell him all about your little accident?"

He must have thought I was another one of Mike Neeland's boys. He shook his head quickly. "No, sir. Not a word to anybody. Nobody at all. I swear it."

"And you don't know anything about Sam Gordon?"

The name set him off like one of Pavlov's conditioned dogs. Wherever it still could, color drained from his face and his voice trembled up the scale. "I never heard of him, mister. Honest. I swear on the Bible."

I doubted if he'd seen a Bible in ten years, but he wasn't the type who will work at keeping a secret if things get uncomfortable.

I took Gordon's photograph out of my pocket. "Do you know him?"

He nodded eagerly. "Sure. That's Ernie."

"Ernie what?"

"Ernie Wallace." Baini's eyes flickered with a sudden fox-like intelligence. "Do other people know him as Sam Gordon?"

I took the snap away from him. "Just tell me what you know about Ernie. Don't keep anything to yourself. You may have had a rough time, but things could get worse. I have a lot more imagination than the people you met last week."

He spoke fast to keep me from being tempted. "I don't know practically nothing about Ernie. We just played pool at Swenson's. Me and Ben and Fitz. We only knew Ernie for a couple of weeks. He never even told us where he lived."

"Did he ever mention what he did for a living?"

"No. I didn't ask. You don't ask questions like that around here."

"And what do you and Ben and Fitz do for a living?"

He stirred uneasily. "Just anything that comes along. Twenty bucks here, thirty there."

"Anything that doesn't take work?"

He nodded.

"When you picked up that package, the one that made you so much unhappiness last week, what did you think was in it?"

"I don't know," he said hastily. "I don't think about things like that. I just follow orders."

"You weren't even tempted to peek?"

"No, sir. You don't do anything like that. You don't cross the big boys." He wiped some of the sweat from his face. "We just run errands like. Me and Ben and Fitz. Or maybe we use muscle on somebody. We get a phone call telling us to do something and we don't ask questions. And in the next day's mail we get twenty, thirty bucks. Sometimes fifty."

"Did Ernie know about how you three picked up your spending money?"

Baini shrugged. "I suppose he could pick up the information somehow. Maybe we let a word go here and there."

"Where can I find Fitz and Ben? And what about their last names?"

"They hang around Swenson's most of the day. That's a bar up the street. Ben Grady and Fitz—Fitz that's Fitz's last name. They got rooms somewhere in the neighborhood, but I don't know exactly where."

Baini flinched as I lit a cigarette, obviously thinking of it as an instrument of torture.

I smiled. "You won't tell anybody I was here?"

"No, mister. Nobody at all." He shook his head almost sorrowfully. "I don't know nothing about anything."

I took my car a block and a half down the street. Swenson's was a tired old-fashioned saloon with bad lighting and a lazy clean-up man. Last night's cigarette butts were still stamped flat on the floor. It was the kind of a place that used to have sawdust on the floor and a family entrance. But that was twenty years ago and times and neighborhoods change.

I ordered a shot and a beer chaser.

Two beat-up tables and some chairs were along one wall.

The pool table was busy in a four-way game of eight ball.

The bar mirror let me know that I was being sized up. My suit told the cueboys that I was either a tourist who happened to get lost in this part of town or maybe I was somebody with business for one of them.

I changed my mind about asking questions and names here. They would make my face remembered and I didn't go for that.

I killed the shot and left.

Across the street I moved into a cafe. The counterman took the toothpick out of his mouth—so he could listen better, I suppose.

"Coffee," I said and walked by him to the telephone booth. I dialed Swenson's Bar.

There was a click as somebody picked up the receiver. "Swenson."

"I'd like to talk to Ben Grady."

"He's not here. Haven't seen him in three, four days."

"Send Fitz to the phone."

There was thirty seconds of silence and then a younger voice took it up. "Fitz talking."

"I got a little work for you."

"Who is this? Tony?"

"No. But I'm talking for him. It's worth thirty bucks. No sweat."

He hesitated. "How's Tony's—ah—stiff arm? Bothering him a lot, I mean?"

The man was exercising his little brain. A hundred to one Tony had oil in all his hinges. "Cut that," I snapped. "We both know that Tony's as limber as they come."

Fitz was apologetic. "Just checking. What do you want me to do?"

"Go to your place and wait one hour. Somebody may or may not bring you a package. He'll tell you what to do with it."

"May or may not?"

"That's right. It all depends on how things work on this

end. But don't worry your head about it. You'll find the thirty in your mail tomorrow."

He might have wanted to ask more questions, but he didn't try. I was one of the big boys to him and you did just as you were told.

I went back to my coffee and watched Swenson's until a square-faced, light-complexioned kid left the place. He was not much over twenty-one. He adjusted his snap brim and began walking west.

I tossed a dime on the counter and left. I gave Fitz a block and a half and followed on the other side of the street.

After four blocks he turned into a grimy three-story apartment building. When I got there I stepped inside and checked the mail slots. Fitz's apartment was number 31.

I went on to a drugstore and bought an envelope and a stamp. I slipped thirty dollars into the envelope and addressed it to Fitz. I didn't want him to lose faith in telephone calls. I thought he might be getting another one soon.

In the phone booth at one end of the store I dialed the Parakeet and got through to Mike Neeland. "You'd better put that ad in the Lost and Found."

Neeland swore softly. "You didn't come up with anything?"

"I'm still working, but I won't come up with anything before five."

Neeland gave it thought. "Maybe we can think up something. How about following whoever picks up the package this time?"

"I wouldn't monkey around, Mike. They probably thought of that, too. If something goes wrong this time, I think they might decide to steer you into the kind of trouble you don't want. Just so they get something out of the whole caper."

He cursed again. "I hate to part with the two hundred thousand, but what really burns is that some punks are getting away with it."

"You don't have a choice right now, Mike. Dorothy Gordon will phone the police in fifteen minutes."

Neeland gave up. "All right. I'll call her and tell her I've decided to pay the money."

There wasn't anything more for me to do now but wait. I took in a movie that night and slept late the next morning.

In the afternoon Mike phoned me at my hotel room.

"I got the two hundred thousand and now I'm waiting. No word yet."

"You probably won't have to deliver until it's nice and dark. When did the ad appear?"

"The eleven-o'clock edition this morning."

"They'll probably phone tonight and at the last minute. That way they won't be giving you any time to build up any tricks."

"I'm not building any tricks," Neeland said gloomily. "I just want to get this over with."

"Call me the minute you get word."

It was a long wait and Neeland finally phoned at ten that night.

"They just got in touch with me."

"By phone?"

"No. Telegram." He laughed softly. "Looks nice and innocent. WILL CALL FOR MY PACKAGE AT 57 AND CC ELEVEN TONIGHT."

I waited until quarter to eleven and then drove to Fitz's apartment building. On the third floor I knocked softly on door 31. Fitz wasn't the kind to spend evenings at home— especially not this one—but I wanted to be positive.

When there was no answer, I went through my ring of keys until I found one that worked.

I closed the door behind me and switched on the lights.

It was a small one room utility apartment with a kitchenette and bath. The pull-down bed was a mess of sheets and blankets and took up almost all of the room. Racing forms almost crowded the telephone off the tiny table at the window. The kitchenette itself was cluttered with dishes and the bathroom was dark with the grime of weeks.

I switched off the lights, sat down on the unmade bed, and lit a cigarette.

When you want someone to pick up a package containing two hundred thousand dollars, you don't just pick a name out of a telephone book. You have to find one of the people who are willing to do that kind of work—and do it without curiosity. You have to find someone who is used to doing things without asking questions, who follows instructions.

You go to the places where you are most likely to find him and his friends. You don't go as Sam Gordon. You go as Ernie Wallace. You play pool with them. You listen. And at last, maybe after weeks, you decide which of them you can trust—for your purposes. Baini, for instance. Or Ben Grady, or Fitz.

You use Baini the first time. But he gets himself caught and he's out of commission.

Now you have another chance at the two hundred thousand. You can't take a risk on a complete stranger as your errand boy. So you come back to Ben and Fitz.

But Ben isn't available—according to whoever had answered the phone at Swenson's—and so that leaves you with Fitz.

I wondered whose fingers those had been. Some bum off the streets? Somebody who wouldn't be missed while he was being cut up? Or maybe they were Ben Grady's. Was he the unlucky patsy? Maybe that was why the fellow at Swenson's hadn't seen him recently.

At eleven-twenty, the phone purred.

When I picked it up, I said, "Fitz."

The voice was a whisper. "Did you get the package?"

So Gordon was really impatient. "Yeah," I said.

There was a little silence. "Any trouble?"

"No."

"Anybody follow you?"

"No." So Gordon hadn't been watching at the pickup point. He was playing it a little different this time.

A little more silence and then, "Take it to the Northwestern Railroad Depot and wait near the ticket island."

I tried to keep my voice as neutral as I could and hoped it would pass as Fitz's. "You'll be there?"

"I might be. Or you might get a phone call telling you where to go from there."

The whisper made the voice impossible to identify. Not that I expected to be able to do that in the first place. I'd never seen or heard Gordon.

"I'm leaving right away," I said, and waited.

The click broke the connection.

I put down the phone. I had a pretty good idea of what was supposed to happen next. Gordon might be at the Northwestern Depot, but I doubted it. Probably there would be another phone call at the station telling Fitz to take the briefcase to some other nice public place. Gordon might pick it up there, but more likely Fitz would be sent on and on, from one place to another. Somewhere along the line Gordon would be waiting—making absolutely sure that Fitz wasn't being followed before he claimed the briefcase.

I lit a cigarette and waited.

At eleven-thirty, I heard the footsteps and then a key being worked in the lock. I went into the bathroom and waited until the lights were on and the door closed. Then I stepped out again.

Fitz's mouth dropped at the sight of me—and the .38.

"No noise," I said. "And everything will be just dandy."

I don't think he could have made any noise at the time anyway. His eyes were hypnotized by the gun.

"Put the briefcase on the bed."

He looked at it as though he had never seen it before and then did as he was told.

"Do you know what's in there?" I asked.

He was rapid to deny it. "No, sir. I don't know a thing about it and I'm not curious."

"And besides, it's locked?"

"Yes, sir. But I wouldn't have looked anyway."

I ran my hands over him to see if he were carrying anything that could hurt me. Then I put away my revolver. I could handle Fitz if he tried anything. "Take it easy."

"Yes, sir." His kind are always polite when they're scared.

I pried the screwdriver blade out of my pocket knife and went to work on the briefcase. I had to be positive that the money was there before I went on with anything else. I don't like to waste effort or take chances for nothing.

I broke the lock and opened the case. It was all there in neat bundles—two hundred thousand dollars.

Fitz watched bug-eyed. "Is it real?"

I hoped it was and I didn't have any reason to doubt it. I looked at Fitz and decided on the next step. If it worked, things would be easier for me. I like to keep them relaxed. "No," I said. "It's counterfeit. You couldn't fool the old lady in the candy store with the stuff."

He stared at me.

I smiled. "The syndicate was testing you. I wanted to know if you could be trusted." I didn't know if there was a syndicate in this city or not, but punks like Fitz always think there is.

The word "syndicate" was like "Major League" to a rookie with the Green Bay Blue Jays. Fitz swallowed. "The syndicate?"

"That's right. We've had our eye on you for quite awhile now."

He didn't know yet whether that was good or bad.

"We think you're ready for bigger things."

He brightened considerably.

"We think you've got what it takes. Not like Grady or Baini."

He was eager to agree with me. "Just small-time pool jockeys."

"That's right. But you've got brains."

Very few people plead innocent when they're accused of having intelligence. Fitz nodded. "It takes brains to get ahead nowadays."

He used those bird brains to ask me a question. "Are you the one who's supposed to pick up the briefcase?"

I smiled. "Was I supposed to give a password or something square like that?"

Fitz shook his head. "No. I just got the phone call. I didn't know who it was, but I was told to pick up the briefcase and bring it back to my room. Somebody would pick it up in the next twenty-four hours."

I clicked my tongue. "That Georgie. He gets twenty thousand a year besides the bonuses and he messes up a simple little thing like this. The least he could have done was to describe me." I picked up the briefcase and went to the door. As a seeming afterthought, I turned. "You got anything planned for the rest of the night?"

"No, sir."

I let him see that I was thinking. I rubbed my jaw. "I think you're ready. Care to see the district boss?"

His mind must have latched on to the twenty grand Georgie was supposed to be making. "Sure. Sure. Anything you say."

I let him carry the briefcase down to the car and he walked as proud as a dog with a newspaper in his mouth.

He almost patted my car as he got in. "Swell heap," he said. He was buying one like that already.

I eased away from the curb. "Turk has his place out in the country."

"Turk?"

"The district boss."

Fitz was imagining. "An estate like?"

"Lots of land. Lot of trees."

The great mind of Fitz was working. "How much does the district boss get?"

"Fifty thousand from the syndicate." I winked. "But anybody who's smart knows how to double that."

Fitz grinned and winked, too. We were buddies and in the know. He got in the car.

It was a pleasant drive, fifteen miles into the country and down a couple of side roads until I found a nice dark stretch of forest.

I stopped the car. "We'll have to walk the rest of the way.

Turk's driveway is being repaved. But there's a path somewhere here right to the house."

We made our way about a hundred yards into the woods
and then I decided that it was time for Fitz's dream to
come to an end.

I had been leading and when I turned I had the .38 in my
hand. In the shadows he might not even have seen it. I fired
once and he dropped without so much as a sound. When
I knelt beside him I saw that one slug had been plenty.

I went back to the car. Gordon would think that Fitz
had double-crossed him and Mike Neeland would think the
same thing about the "kidnapers" of Gordon.

Two hundred thousand dollars was missing and I was the
only one who knew where it was.

Back in the city I got a locker at the bus station and
deposited the briefcase. It was a fine day's work and I was
tempted to leave it at that.

But I began to wonder what Gordon would do now.
When he eventually decided that Fitz had skipped with the
money, would he keep sending more fingers back to Neeland hoping that he could pry another two grand out of
him?

The more I thought about it, the more I saw that there
was still extra change to pick up. Suppose I presented Gordon to Neeland? With all of his ten fingers? I had the idea
that Neeland would be profitably grateful.

I put myself in Gordon's shoes. When I discovered that
Fitz hadn't gone to the Northwestern Railroad Depot, what
would I do? What would I think?

Had Fitz double-crossed me? Had he skipped with the
money? Had he been picked up by Neeland's men? Were
they working on him, hoping for a few enlightening words?

Or would I hope against my suspicions that something
minor had happened? Maybe Fitz's car had broken down.
But then wouldn't the idiot have sense enough to take a
taxi?

I would fret and fume and go through a pack of
cigarettes. Should I go to Fitz's apartment? No. That was

out. Too dangerous. Neeland's men might be waiting for me. Should I go to the railroad station? No. That was no use. I'd had Fitz paged and he couldn't be there.

There wasn't a thing I could do except phone and phone the railroad station again and again. And Fitz's apartment. Would all that phoning do any good? I wouldn't know. But it was better than just sitting and doing nothing.

I drove back to Fitz's apartment and let myself in. I didn't have to wait long. The phone came to life at a quarter to one.

I picked it up and said, "Fitz."

The other end of the line nearly exploded. There was no whispering this time. He was too angry for that. "Where the hell have you been?" he wanted to know.

I'd never met Gordon or heard his voice, but this wasn't him. It sounded like . . . I had to hear the voice talk some more before I could be sure. "I had trouble with my car," I mumbled.

The man's exasperation was overwhelming. "Why the hell didn't you take a taxi?"

I kept talking as though I had cornflakes in my mouth. "I thought it was something that would take just a minute to fix, but it took longer than I thought."

He cursed. "What are you doing back in your apartment?"

"I got dirty, so I'm washing up."

I couldn't see him, but I had the idea that the phone he was holding was in danger of being broken in two.

"Listen, dimwit," he snapped. "Get over to the railroad station. And that means right now."

I placed the voice now. It was Van Camp, Mike Neeland's manager at the Blue Moraine. "You'll be there?" I asked.

"Don't worry about that. Just drag that lead bottom over there and wait."

I put down the phone. It didn't matter to me if Van Camp went there or not. If he did he'd probably be nice and snug in a spot from which he could see me without my seeing him. He might even be making his calls from the Blue

Moraine, planning to send me from place to place before he
made an appearance.

I got to the Blue Moraine forty-five minutes later. It was
the shank of the evening for the kind of entertainment the
club provided, and the fleet of cars parked outside told me
that the second floor was doing a good business.

I asked about Van Camp and wasn't too surprised to find
that he was in.

I went to the rear of the first floor, knocked on the door
marked "Private," and turned the knob.

Van Camp was at his desk. The smoke was thick in the
room and the ashtray sported a mound of butts.

Van Camp glared at me irritably. "What do you want?"

I closed the door behind me. "It's all over, Van Camp."

"What are you talking about?"

"I have a good ear for voices. You weren't talking to Fitz
a little while ago. You were talking to me."

His eyes narrowed warily. "Who is Fitz supposed to be?"

I smiled. "Baini, Ben Grady, and Fitz were what you
might call your reservoir of messenger boys. You sent Baini
out the first time and he got messed up. That left you with
Ben and Fitz. Ben, I understand, is out of town. And that
left you only Fitz. Simple, no? I figured it out with my own
little brain."

"You're talking through your hat." But the curiosity got
him just the same. "This Fitz you're talking about. Where is
he?"

I don't know if I managed a blush, but I tried. "I don't
know. I waited for him and finally forced my way into his
apartment. It looks like he just picked up the briefcase and
kept traveling."

Van Camp's face got splotched with anger, but he said
nothing.

I moved my hand significantly into my pocket. "I may
have missed Fitz, but I've got you."

He still wasn't admitting anything. "And what do you
expect out of that?"

"I think Mike Neeland might get a little satisfaction out of talking to you. Know what I mean?"

He didn't like the thought of that. He made a big operation out of selecting a cigarette out of the silver casket on his desk. "How much is Neeland paying you?"

"I'm expecting five thousand."

Van Camp decided to stop being coy. "I'll give you ten."

I shook my head. "I wouldn't buck Neeland. He's got too many friends."

"Twenty," Van Camp said.

"Not for double that." I sighed. "Even if I would, you're trying to buy out with Confederate money. If you had twenty grand, you wouldn't be messing around with kidnaping." I waited for something more concrete. I wondered if I would have to suggest it myself.

The faint shine of perspiration appeared on Van Camp's forehead. "Look, I'm the manager of this place," he said. "Right? Every evening we take in twenty, thirty grand."

"Not your money," I said.

He was explaining something to a backward boy— patiently, but desperately. "But I get to handle it for awhile. Mike doesn't send his collector to pick up the receipts until six in the morning."

I played it dense. "What are you going to tell Mike when he finds money missing?"

"I won't tell him anything," Van Camp snapped impatiently. "By six I'll be out of the state and still going."

I finally nodded, "Let's see the money."

Van Camp had some of it in his safe and he went around to the play on the second floor and got as much more as he could without crippling the tables or raising eyebrows. I followed him when he did that. Not so close that anybody would remember we were together, but close enough so that he wouldn't get the idea of pocketing the money himself and jet-planing out a rear door.

Back in his office, we totaled up and had something in the neighborhood of eighteen thousand.

Van Camp was sweating with the exertion of it all, as he

shoveled the money into a briefcase and handed it to me.

"What about Gordon?" I asked.

He was a trifle irritated to be reminded of Gordon at this particular time. "Let him die there."

The words made me blink. "Where is he?"

I got him tied up in the cellar of a little cottage I own up in the mountains."

I put the briefcase under my arm and decided that it wouldn't hurt to display a little real ignorance now. "I thought you and Gordon were in on this together."

"We were." He glanced at his watch, eager to be off into the wild blue yonder. "Gordon was the one who scouted out Baini, Grady, and Fitz. But after the first drop didn't work, he was all in favor of pulling out and forgetting the whole thing."

It came to me clear now. "But you didn't go for that? And the fingers really belonged to Gordon?"

He nodded. The matter no longer interested him. He was thinking of other things.

"You'll have to get rid of Gordon," I said. "Right now."

"Why bother? He'll die right where he is in a couple of days without food or water."

"Maybe. But suppose he should get away? He might be just mean enough to go to the police and make out like it was a real kidnaping. The fingers he's got missing will make his story hold real water. And then you'll wind up with not only Neeland after you, but the whole F.B.I. You wouldn't stand a chance." I let that sink in. "If you're a little squeamish about applying the final touch, I'll do it for you."

Van Camp saw it my way, but not happily. "All right. But let's hurry it up."

We took his car and it was a forty-five minute trip, even at the fast clip we were going. We finally turned into what looked like an old logging road and pulled up in front of the cottage at three in the morning.

Van Camp got out of the car with a flashlight and I

followed him. The small frame building was without electricity and smelled of dust. In the kitchen Van Camp reached down for a ring set in the linoleum-covered floor.

He pulled open the trap door and the beam of his flashlight cut down into the mouldy darkness. The cellar was hardly more than a hole in the ground and Gordon lay in one corner, his hands tied behind him. He was gagged and the rope wound around his feet was looped around his neck. Anyway you looked at it, he wasn't getting much air.

Gordon didn't look pretty now and his eyes were shiny with terror.

"Get it over with," Van Camp commanded.

I didn't bother to go down the wooden steps. I fired once. Gordon jerked with the impact of the bullet and rolled over on his face. I saw that two fingers of his right hand were missing. And that told me something.

Van Camp was about to lower the trap door.

"I'm not through yet," I said.

His eyes went to mine and he had about one second to realize what was going to happen next.

My slug caught him true and as he staggered I gave him a slight push with my fingertips. He dropped down into the hole and the flashlight rolled in too before I could stop it. I closed the trap door and used my lighter to find my way out of the cottage.

I drove back to the Blue Moraine, picked up my own car, and got back to the city by five o'clock. The sun was just beginning to come up.

I found an all-night cafe and had a slow breakfast. Then I deposited the eighteen grand in my locker at the bus depot and went to my hotel room for a few self-inflicted congratulatory drinks.

At six-thirty, I drove to the Parakeet. The games were closed down now and the help gone. In an hour or so the cleanup crew would show up for work.

Mike Neeland was still in his office. His eyes were circled with fatigue. "Something's gone wrong, Danny. They haven't let Gordon go yet. His wife called me just fifteen minutes ago. She says she's going to phone the police if I don't see that he's released right away."

I lit a cigarette. "Mike, I've put all the pieces together. I'm sorry it's too late for me to do anything about things, but—"

"What are you talking about?"

"The kidnaping," I said. "It wasn't a kidnaping at all. Gordon's still got all ten of his fingers and he's a long way from here by now."

Neeland's eyes narrowed.

"The fingers probably belonged to some poor bum Gordon picked up. Gordon planned this whole shakedown." I thought for a moment about the eight fingers Gordon still had when I had seen him last. I knew the answer to the question I asked. "Did you get another finger in the mail yesterday?"

"No."

"But you *should* have."

He frowned. "Why? I already agreed to pay."

I smiled. "According to the postmarks on the wrappers, Gordon mailed the first two fingers from places thirty to forty miles away. His notes promised steady delivery. Your ad telling him that you were going to meet his terms didn't appear in the *Journal* until the eleven-o'clock morning edition. And so if he depended exclusively on that ad for all his information, he should *already* have had another finger on its way in time for you to get it in your one-thirty mail."

I paused. "But he already knew that the ad was going to appear. He knew it the day before. He didn't have to bother cutting off another finger that night and mailing it. He knew that you were going to pay because somebody *told* him. And who knew the ad was going to appear? Just you, and me—and Dorothy Gordon."

And that's the way it was. Except that it was Van Camp, Dorothy Gordon had told. Not Sam Gordon. And I had the idea that a woman who would let her husband be cut to bits had other plans. Probably she and Van Camp had decided to kill Gordon after they got the money and go away together.

Mike Neeland paced my information back and forth across the room.

"There's something else," I said. "I think that Gordon took the money and ran off without his wife."

"What makes you think that?"

"You told me she just phoned. Now would she do that if Gordon *and* she had the money?" I shook my head. "No. She thinks you didn't pay. But eventually she'll get onto the fact that he ran off."

Neeland swore thoroughly. Then he glared at me. "I want you to take care of Dorothy Gordon right away. Get that?"

I nodded. "All right, Mike. And I'll do that errand for nothing. I haven't done you much good on this job."

He waved that away. "No. I'll see that you get the usual five grand for it."

The phone rang and Neeland picked it up. As he listened his face got even darker. Finally, he slammed down the receiver.

I waited politely.

Neeland breathed hard. "On top of everything else, it looks like Van Camp emptied the till at the Blue Moraine and skipped. I suppose he's in South America too by now."

I rose and put on my hat. "I'll take care of Dorothy Gordon now."

He stopped me at the door. "Danny."

"Yes?"

"Danny, when you take care of that, come back here."

"Sure. I'll report back in."

"That isn't what I mean, Danny. I'd like you to stay with me. In the organization."

I thought about the organization—about the eighteen thousand the Blue Moraine took in by only two in the morning, about the other clubs Mike owned.

And I thought about Eve Neeland too.

I met his eyes. "I once heard you say that you didn't want anybody with brains around you."

He smiled faintly. "Sure you got brains, Danny, but there's something more about you."

"What's that?"

His face became solemn. "I can trust you. That's what."

Tears didn't come to my eyes, but I did let him see me swallow. "Thanks, boss. You can count on me."

Over Eight Months on
The New York Times Bestseller List

ARMAGEDDON
Leon Uris

A magnificent novel of Berlin in the grim, turbulent days immediately after World War II, by the author of EXODUS and BATTLE CRY. The struggle for power among the victors, culminating in the breathtaking drama of the Berlin Airlift.

"A vast panorama of people and places . . ."
—New York Herald Tribune

A DELL BOOK   **95c**

Over Four Months on
The New York Times Bestseller List.

FUNERAL
IN BERLIN

LEN DEIGHTON

A crackling tale of espionage which takes
the reader from London to Prague, from a
beach in Spain to the streets of Berlin. The
author brings vividly to life the nightmare
world of faceless men caught in the power
struggles of the countries they represent.

". . . a highly readable and engaging
tale . . ." —Los Angeles Times

A DELL BOOK   75c

If you cannot obtain copies of these titles at your local newsstand, just send
the price (plus 10c per copy for handling and postage) to Dell Books, Box
2291, Grand Central Post Office, New York, N.Y. 10017. No postage or handling
charge is required on any order of five or more books.